GRAY

Poetry

&

Prose

AMS PRESS
NEW YORK

Library of Congress Cataloging in Publication Data

Gray, Thomas, 1716-1771.
  Gray, poetry & prose.

  Reprint of the 1926 ed. published by the Clarendon
Press, Oxford.
    1. Gray, Thomas, 1716-1771—Correspondence.
2. Poets, English—18th century—Correspondence.
I. Crofts, John Ernest Victor, 1887—   II. Title.
PR3501.C7   1979   821'.6   76-29472 ✓
ISBN 0-404-15304-6

First AMS edition published in 1979.

Reprinted from the edition of 1926, Oxford. [Trim size and text
area of the original have been slightly altered in this edition.
Original trim size: 12.2 × 18.2 cm; text area: 9.4 × 15.2 cm.]

The frontispiece is from the portrait
of Gray by John Giles Eckardt in
the National Portrait Gallery

THOMAS GRAY

G R A Y,

Poetry & Prose,

With Essays by
JOHNSON, GOLDSMITH
and others

Gray, Thomas

With an Introduction and Notes by

J. CROFTS

OXFORD
AT THE CLARENDON PRESS
1926

Printed in England
At the OXFORD UNIVERSITY PRESS
By John Johnson
Printer to the University

CONTENTS

CONTENTS

INTRODUCTION

' I HATE a fellow ', said Johnson, ' whom pride or
cowardice or laziness drives into a corner, and who does
nothing when he is there but sit and growl ; let him come
out as I do and bark.'

Gray never did that. ' In London ', says Rogers, ' he
saw little Society ; had a nice dinner from the Tavern
brought to his rooms, a glass or two of Sweet wine, and as
he sipped it talked about great People.'

Some such mental portrait of Gray must always have
been in Johnson's mind.

' He attacked Gray,' says Boswell, ' calling him a dull
fellow.

Boswell. I understood he was reserved and might appear
dull in company ; but sure he was not dull in poetry.

Johnson. Sir, he was dull in company, dull in his closet,
dull everywhere. He was dull in a new way, and that
made people think him great.'

Nothing could be more perverse, and yet, no doubt, it
was inevitable. For quite apart from superficial manner-
isms, the very texture of Gray's thought and sentiment
must always have been uncongenial to Johnson. The
tender, shallow, and somewhat wilful melancholy of the
Elegy, with its facile philosophy and gentle egotism, can
never have appealed much to one who ' hated ', as he told
Hannah More, ' to hear people whine about metaphysical
distresses when there is so much want and hunger in the
world ' : a world, as he said on another occasion, ' bursting
with sin and sorrow '.

If Gray had shown any real sense of this, even at the
expense of his poetry ; if his *Elegy* had been a poem like

Crabbe's *Village*, bleached and corroded by the writer's sense of ' the miseries of the world ', Johnson would have thought better of the man and, probably, of the poet. But the *Elegy*, after all, is a complacent piece. It contains none of that wild trouble which took shape in *The Old Leech Gatherer*. The rude forefathers of Gray's hamlet are at best a pageant of shadows, devised to grace the imagined obsequies of a poet ; they draw the tears that are to bedew another's grave ; and the meaning of the poem is not complete until we have passed from the real to the fictitious, and stand gazing at the hypothetical epitaph of a hypothetical youth.

' Surely ', says Johnson testily in his life of Cowley, ' it is not difficult in the solitude of a College, or the bustle of the world, to find useful studies and serious employment. No man needs to be so burthened with life as to squander it in dreams of fictitious occurrences.' Yet he praises the *Elegy* ; and praises it in terms which show that his enjoyment of the poetry and his sense of justice could triumph over his distaste for the poet.

The *Life of Gray* provoked several pamphlets in the poet's defence. But although many of Johnson's verdicts were reversed by the critics of the succeeding generation, his estimate of Gray was not seriously challenged.

' Johnson has been abused ', says a writer in the *London Magazine* for 1822, ' more perhaps for undervaluing the merits of Gray than for any of his offences against literature. For our own parts we think that he has been abused unjustly. Were we to cast a stone at him it would be for his life of Milton. But Gray has of all poets in the language the least right to complain. His reputation is enormously too great for the foundation upon which it rests. No doubt that he had learning and a pleasant way of communicating his thoughts. But his language is beyond even that of his contemporaries artificial ; and his poems are not

remarkable either for original thought or even felicity of expression. His *Elegy* is clearly the first of his compositions;
there is a tender vein of melancholy running through it;
and the reflections generally speaking, if not very profound,
are graceful and pleasing.'

Goldsmith's forecast of the fate of the *Odes* had, on the
whole, been justified by the event. They had acquired,
it is true, some notoriety as specimens of ' the sublime '
during the closing years of the century. But that was the
age of what Professor Legouis felicitously calls ' le culte
d'écharpements ', and a modish taste for ' sublimity ' was
common. The same wave of fashion elevated for a moment
such miscellaneous objects as Macpherson's *Ossian*,
Falconer's *Shipwreck*, and the *Odes* of Mason; submerged
Rembrandt; exalted Salvator Rosa; and having deposited
a jetsam of tourists among the Cumbrian mountains, and
a series of marble statesmen in togas about our public
walks, broke, foamed, and evaporated upon the vast
canvases of Benjamin Haydon. When it was all over,
Gray's *Odes* were found to be exactly where Goldsmith
had placed them : not an inch farther up the beach.
Cowper, perplexed in his search for English words to translate the sublime language of Homer, might find them
suggestive, and praise them with characteristic generosity;
but Coleridge found them ' frigid and artificial '; Lamb
boggled over their confusions of metaphor; Hazlitt was
content to ' give them up '.

To Wordsworth, as to Johnson, Gray's poetry was on
the whole a storehouse of ' gaudy and inane phraseology ';
but he went farther than Johnson in the moral inferences
that he drew. Johnson disliked Gray because he pictured
him as unfitted for ordinary social intercourse ; Wordsworth
because he fancied him fit for nothing else. He regarded
him as the mouthpiece of those ' false refinements ' and
' effeminate habits of thinking and feeling ' which in the

last age had passed for a polite taste ; and he divined that by the mysterious witchcraft in language Gray's lip-service had ended in a real servitude of the spirit. ' The true and the false ', he says in the famous Appendix, ' were inseparably interwoven until, the taste of men becoming gradually perverted, this language was received as a natural language, and at length by the influence of books upon men did to a certain degree really become so.' It is not, therefore, for his meretricious diction alone that Wordsworth looks askance at Gray, but because the habit of falsity seemed to have touched his heart ; because he could not even write the epitaph of the mother whom he dearly loved without being betrayed into insincerity of thought and feeling.

But after all, where language itself is inadequate a convention is inevitable, and its nature will be determined by contemporary usage. Gray belonged to the age of ' decorum and Chesterfield ' when it was permissible not merely to affect real feeling in order to conceal self-consciousness, but (more subtly) to affect self-consciousness in order to conceal real feeling. That he was not the ' thwart, disnatured ' character that Wordsworth's tirade in the *Essay on Epitaphs* would make him out, is abundantly evident in his correspondence. His letters present a portrait not merely of the sensitive and melancholy scholar, familiar to readers of Johnson's *Life*, but of a merry and whimsical companion, a warm-hearted, even a passionate friend, and (what is more surprising) of a nature-lover who could look as steadily at his subject as Wordsworth himself.

It is perhaps because Hazlitt seems to have approached Gray through his letters that his sketch presents a truer estimate. Where Johnson applies a rigid common sense, and Wordsworth stern moral principles, Hazlitt allows his sense of humour to play upon the subject ; and his pleasant miniature of Gray as the youth who never grew up, though a trifle too rosy in tint, is something better than caricature.

Gray never lost the sensibility and freshness of interest that are associated with youth. What he did lose, or perhaps never fully acquired, was the mental hardiness without which these gifts must remain sterile. No one can read his letters without wondering how the harvest of so rich a mind could be so small, or without suspecting the defect of character at which Hazlitt seems to hint. ' What a happiness,' he cries, never to be ' anything more than a looker on! '—and we hear the solemn echo of my Lord Verulam's ' Men must know that in this mortal life it is reserved for God and the angels to be lookers on '.

It is a relief to turn from critics who busy themselves about Gray's personality to one who disregards it almost entirely. Campbell did not appreciate Gray's humour, having little or none himself; but he did appreciate at their proper value the qualities of Gray's serious poetry, because he had sought to attain many of them in his own. He is therefore a sympathetic critic in the special sense that he understands quite clearly what Gray is trying to do in poetry. And this is important. It is for lack of such sympathy that later criticism has sometimes become fanciful and misleading. Matthew Arnold, for instance, extends his urbane compassion to Gray as a poet born in an age of prose; but he deserves it rather as one dying on the eve of a poetic typhoon that obliterated all the standards and ideals by which he had worked. For among the rhapsodists, lispers, shock-headed dreamers, and poets *in querpo* who were preparing to sing the praises of the poetical Reformation Gray stands forth as the last champion of Apostolic Succession. Not a phrase of his poetry but has its sanction in some earlier usage; hardly a thought but wears the escutcheon of a noble house. The rhetorical forms and verbal ceremonies—the ' linen decency ' of language—which to his successors seemed the symbol of a creed outworn, were to Gray of the very substance of his faith ; and wrapped in his gorgeous singing-robes he moves through the ancient ritual, like the last faithful priest in a conquered city. Poetry for him was no sudden grace or fluttering gift of tongues. It was a spiritual and verbal inheritance, a treasury of merits, continually re-endowed by every high thought and noble expression. For a man to pretend that he could stand without it, that the wealth of his nature could dispense with the inheritance of art, and that he could weave from his own poor substance a poetical tissue richer than that to which the immortals had contributed their gold, would have seemed to Gray impudent and profane. Had he lived to see the rise of such a heresy, he would have given up poetry altogether.

LIFE OF GRAY

1716, Dec. 26. Born in Cornhill, London.

1727–34. At Eton. Becomes intimate with Horace Walpole, Richard West, and Thomas Ashton.

1734, Oct.–1738, Sept. Pensioner of Peterhouse, Cambridge. (Walpole at Trinity College, Cambridge, 1735–9, West at Christ Church, Oxford, 1735–8.)

1738. In London at his father's house. (West at the Inner Temple.)

1739–41. Tour with Walpole in France and Italy.

1741. Quarrel and parting with Walpole at Reggio (April). Visits Venice, and returns to London (September). Death of his father, Nov. 6.

1742. Returns to Cambridge as Fellow Commoner of Peterhouse. Death of Richard West, June 1.

1744. Takes the degree of B.C.L.

1745. Reconciled with Walpole.

1747. *Ode on a Distant Prospect of Eton College* published by Dodsley (anonymous).

1748. *On the Spring* and *On the Death of a Favourite Cat* published in Dodsley's *Miscellany*, vol. ii (anonymous), along with the *Eton College* Ode. Makes the acquaintance of the Rev. William Mason.

1751. *Elegy Written in a Country Churchyard* published by Dodsley (anonymous).

1753. Death of his mother, March 14.

Designs by Mr. R. Bentley for Six Poems by Mr. T. Gray (the odes already in print, the *Elegy*, the *Hymn to Adversity*, and *A Long Story*) published by Dodsley.

1753. Visits Dr. Wharton at Durham, July–September.

1754. Makes a tour in Northamptonshire and Warwickshire.

1756. Removes from Peterhouse to Pembroke College, Cambridge.

1757. *Odes by Mr. Gray* (*The Progress of Poesy* and *The Bard*) printed by Walpole at Strawberry Hill.
Refuses the Laureateship.

1761. Meets Norton Nicholls.

1765. Makes a tour in Scotland with Lord Strathmore; meets Robertson and 'other literati' at Edinburgh, and Beattie at Glamis Castle.

1767. Spends six months in York and Durham, visiting Mason and Dr. Wharton.

1768. *Poems by Mr. Gray* (all the poems here reprinted except those on pp. 66–8) published in London by Dodsley and in Glasgow by Foulis.

Appointed Regius Professor of Modern History at Cambridge, and made a Fellow of Pembroke College.

1769. *Ode for Music* performed at the Installation of the Duke of Grafton as Chancellor of the University of Cambridge.
Visits Dr. Wharton and makes a tour in the Lake District.

1771. Dies at Cambridge, July 30 ; buried at Stoke Poges.

CHIEF EDITIONS

The Poems of Mr. Gray. To which are prefixed Memoirs of his Life and Writings by W. Mason. York, 1775 (second edition, London, 1775).

[130 letters are included in the Memoirs.]

Works, ed. T. J. Mathias, 2 vols., 1814.

Works, ed. John Mitford, 2 vols., 1816 ; 4 vols., 1836 (vol. v. 1843).

Works, ed. Edmund Gosse, 4 vols., 1884.

Poetical Works, ed. John Bradshaw (New Aldine Edition), 1891.

Letters of Thomas Gray, ed. Duncan C. Tovey, 3 vols., 1909–12.

[Contains 388 letters.]

The Correspondence of Gray, Walpole, West, and Ashton, 1734–1771, ed. Paget Toynbee, 2 vols., 1915.

[Contains over 100 letters hitherto unpublished.]

Poetical Works, ed. A. L. Poole (Oxford edition), 1917.

[Contains the fullest record of variant readings.]

JOHNSON'S
Life of Gray

Published 1781

THOMAS GRAY, the son of Mr. Philip Gray, a scrivener of London, was born in Cornhill, November 26, 1716. His grammatical education he received at Eton under the care of Mr. Antrobus, his mother's brother, then assistant to Dr. George, and when he left school, in 1734, entered a pensioner at Peterhouse in Cambridge.

The transition from the school to the college is, to most young scholars, the time from which they date their years of manhood, liberty, and happiness; but Gray seems to have been very little delighted with academical gratifica- 10 tions; he liked at Cambridge neither the mode of life nor the fashion of study, and lived sullenly on to the time when his attendance on lectures was no longer required. As he intended to profess the Common Law, he took no degree.

When he had been at Cambridge about five years, Mr. Horace Walpole, whose friendship he had gained at Eton, invited him to travel with him as his companion. They wandered through France into Italy; and Gray's letters contain a very pleasing account of many parts of their journey. But unequal friendships are easily dissolved: 20 at Florence they quarrelled, and parted; and Mr. Walpole is now content to have it told that it was by his fault. If we look however without prejudice on the world, we shall find that men, whose consciousness of their own merit sets them above the compliances of servility, are apt enough in their association with superiors to watch their own dignity with troublesome and punctilious jealousy, and in the fervour of independence to exact that attention which they refuse to pay. Part they did, whatever was the quarrel, and the rest of their travels was doubtless more unpleasant to them both. Gray continued his journey in a manner suitable to his own little fortune, with only an occasional servant.

He returned to England in September 1741, and in about two months afterwards buried his father; who had, by an
10 injudicious waste of money upon a new house, so much lessened his fortune that Gray thought himself too poor to study the law. He therefore retired to Cambridge, where he soon after became Bachelor of Civil Law; and where, without liking the place or its inhabitants, or professing to like them, he passed, except a short residence at London, the rest of his life.

About this time he was deprived of Mr. West, the son of a chancellor of Ireland, a friend on whom he appears to have set a high value, and who deserved his esteem by the
20 powers which he shews in his Letters, and in the *Ode to May*, which Mr. Mason has preserved, as well as by the sincerity with which, when Gray sent him part of *Agrippina*, a tragedy that he had just begun, he gave an opinion which probably intercepted the progress of the work, and which the judgement of every reader will confirm. It was certainly no loss to the English stage that *Agrippina* was never finished.

In this year (1742) Gray seems to have applied himself seriously to poetry; for in this year were produced the
30 *Ode to Spring*, his *Prospect of Eton*, and his *Ode to Adversity*. He began likewise a Latin poem, *De Principiis Cogitandi*.

It may be collected from the narrative of Mr. Mason, that his first ambition was to have excelled in Latin poetry: perhaps it were reasonable to wish that he had prosecuted

his design ; for though there is at present some embarrass-
ment in his phrase, and some harshness in his Lyric
numbers, his copiousness of language is such as very few
possess, and his lines, even when imperfect, discover a
writer whom practice would quickly have made skilful.

He now lived on at Peterhouse, very little solicitous what
others did or thought, and cultivated his mind and enlarged
his views without any other purpose than of improving
and amusing himself ; when Mr. Mason, being elected
fellow of Pembroke-hall, brought him a companion who 10
was afterwards to be his editor, and whose fondness and
fidelity has kindled in him a zeal of admiration, which
cannot be reasonably expected from the neutrality of
a stranger and the coldness of a critic.

In this retirement he wrote (1747) an ode on the *Death of
Mr. Walpole's Cat*, and the year afterwards attempted
a poem of more importance, on *Government and Education*,
of which the fragments which remain have many excellent
lines.

His next production (1750) was his far-famed *Elegy in the* 20
Church-yard, which, finding its way into a Magazine, first,
I believe, made him known to the public.

An invitation from lady Cobham about this time gave
occasion to an odd composition called *A Long Story*, which
adds little to Gray's character.

Several of his pieces were published (1753), with designs,
by Mr. Bentley ; and, that they might in some form or other
make a book, only one side of each leaf was printed. I
believe the poems and the plates recommended each other
so well, that the whole impression was soon bought. This 30
year he lost his mother.

Some time afterwards (1756) some young men of the
college, whose chambers were near his, diverted themselves
with disturbing him by frequent and troublesome noises,

and, as is said, by pranks yet more offensive and con-
temptuous. This insolence, having endured it a while,
he represented to the governors of the society, among
whom perhaps he had no friends, and, finding his complaint little regarded, removed himself to Pembroke-hall.

In 1757 he published *The Progress of Poetry* and *The Bard*,
two compositions at which the readers of poetry were at
first content to gaze in mute amazement. Some that tried
them confessed their inability to understand them, though
10 Warburton said that they were understood as well as the
works of Milton and Shakespeare, which it is the fashion
to admire. Garrick wrote a few lines in their praise. Some
hardy champions undertook to rescue them from neglect,
and in a short time many were content to be shewn beauties
which they could not see.

Gray's reputation was now so high that, after the death
of Cibber, he had the honour of refusing the laurel, which
was then bestowed on Mr. Whitehead.

His curiosity, not long after, drew him away from Cam-
20 bridge to a lodging near the Museum, where he resided
near three years, reading and transcribing ; and, so far
as can be discovered, very little affected by two odes on
Oblivion and *Obscurity*, in which his Lyric performances
were ridiculed with much contempt and much ingenuity.

When the Professor of Modern History at Cambridge
died, he was, as he says, *cockered and spirited up*, till he
asked it of lord Bute, who sent him a civil refusal ; and
the place was given to Mr. Brocket, the tutor of Sir James
Lowther.

30 His constitution was weak, and believing that his health
was promoted by exercise and change of place, he undertook
(1765) a journey into Scotland, of which his account, so
far as it extends, is very curious and elegant ; for as his
comprehension was ample, his curiosity extended to all the

works of art, all the appearances of nature, and all the
monuments of past events. He naturally contracted a
friendship with Dr. Beattie, whom he found a poet, a
philosopher, and a good man. The Marischal College at
Aberdeen offered him the degree of Doctor of Laws, which,
having omitted to take it at Cambridge, he thought it
decent to refuse.

What he had formerly solicited in vain, was at last given
him without solicitation. The Professorship of History
became again vacant, and he received (1768) an offer of it 10
from the duke of Grafton. He accepted, and retained it
to his death ; always designing lectures, but never reading
them ; uneasy at his neglect of duty, and appeasing his
uneasiness with designs of reformation, and with a resolution which he believed himself to have made of resigning
the office, if he found himself unable to discharge it.

Ill health made another journey necessary, and he visited
(1769) Westmoreland and Cumberland. He that reads his
epistolary narration wishes that to travel, and to tell his
travels, had been more of his employment ; but it is by 20
studying at home that we must obtain the ability of
travelling with intelligence and improvement.

His travels and his studies were now near their end. The
gout, of which he had sustained many weak attacks, fell
upon his stomach, and, yielding to no medicines, produced
strong convulsions, which (July 30, 1771) terminated in
death.

His character I am willing to adopt, as Mr. Mason has
done, from a Letter written to my friend Mr. Boswell, by
the Rev. Mr. Temple, rector of St. Gluvias in Cornwall ; 30
and am as willing as his warmest well-wisher to believe
it true.

' Perhaps he was the most learned man in Europe. He
was equally acquainted with the elegant and profound

parts of science, and that not superficially but thoroughly. He knew every branch of history, both natural and civil; had read all the original historians of England, France, and Italy; and was a great antiquarian. Criticism, metaphysics, morals, politics, made a principal part of his study; voyages and travels of all sorts were his favourite amusements; and he had a fine taste in painting, prints, architecture, and gardening. With such a fund of knowledge, his conversation must have been equally instructing
10 and entertaining; but he was also a good man, a man of virtue and humanity. There is no character without some speck, some imperfection; and I think the greatest defect in his was an affectation in delicacy, or rather effeminacy, and a visible fastidiousness, or contempt and disdain of his inferiors in science. He also had, in some degree, that weakness which disgusted Voltaire so much in Mr. Congreve: though he seemed to value others chiefly according to the progress they had made in knowledge, yet he could not bear to be considered himself merely as a man of letters;
20 and though without birth, or fortune, or station, his desire was to be looked upon as a private independent gentleman, who read for his amusement. Perhaps it may be said, What signifies so much knowledge, when it produced so little? Is it worth taking so much pains to leave no memorial but a few poems? But let it be considered that Mr. Gray was, to others, at least innocently employed; to himself, certainly beneficially. His time passed agreeably; he was every day making some new acquisition in science; his mind was enlarged, his heart softened, his virtue
30 strengthened; the world and mankind were shewn to him without a mask; and he was taught to consider every thing as trifling, and unworthy of the attention of a wise man, except the pursuit of knowledge and practice of virtue, in that state wherein God hath placed us.'

To this character Mr. Mason has added a more particular account of Gray's skill in zoology. He has remarked that Gray's effeminacy was affected most *before those whom he did not wish to please*; and that he is unjustly charged with making knowledge his sole reason of preference, as

he paid his esteem to none whom he did not likewise believe
to be good.

What has occurred to me, from the slight inspection of
his Letters in which my undertaking has engaged me, is
that his mind had a large grasp; that his curiosity was
unlimited, and his judgement cultivated; that he was
a man likely to love much where he loved at all, but that he
was fastidious and hard to please. His contempt however
is often employed, where I hope it will be approved, upon
scepticism and infidelity. His short account of Shaftesbury
I will insert.

'You say you cannot conceive how lord Shaftesbury
came to be a philosopher in vogue; I will tell you: first,
he was a lord; secondly, he was as vain as any of his
readers; thirdly, men are very prone to believe what they
do not understand; fourthly, they will believe any thing
at all, provided they are under no obligation to believe it;
fifthly, they love to take a new road, even when that road
leads no where; sixthly, he was reckoned a fine writer,
and seems always to mean more than he said. Would
you have any more reasons? An interval of above forty
years has pretty well destroyed the charm. A dead lord
ranks with commoners: vanity is no longer interested
in the matter; for a new road is become an old one.'

Mr. Mason has added, from his own knowledge, that
though Gray was poor, he was not eager of money; and that,
out of the little that he had, he was very willing to help
the necessitous.

As a writer he had this peculiarity, that he did not write
his pieces first rudely, and then correct them, but laboured
every line as it arose in the train of composition; and he
had a notion not very peculiar, that he could not write
but at certain times, or at happy moments; a fantastic
foppery, to which my kindness for a man of learning and
of virtue wishes him to have been superior.

GRAY'S Poetry is now to be considered; and I hope not to be looked on as an enemy to his name, if I confess that I contemplate it with less pleasure than his life.

His *Ode on Spring* has something poetical, both in the language and the thought; but the language is too luxuriant, and the thoughts have nothing new. There has of late arisen a practice of giving to adjectives, derived from substantives, the termination of participles, such as the *cultured* plain, the *daisied* bank; but I was sorry to
10 see, in the lines of a scholar like Gray, the *honied* Spring. The morality is natural, but too stale; the conclusion is pretty.

The poem on the *Cat* was doubtless by its author considered as a trifle, but it is not a happy trifle. In the first stanza *the azure flowers* that *blow* shew how resolutely a rhyme is sometimes made when it cannot easily be found. Selima, the Cat, is called a nymph, with some violence both to language and sense; but there is good use made of it when it is done; for of the two lines,

20   What female heart can gold despise ?
             What cat's averse to fish ?

the first relates merely to the nymph, and the second only to the cat. The sixth stanza contains a melancholy truth, that *a favourite has no friend*; but the last ends in a pointed sentence of no relation to the purpose; if *what glistered* had been *gold*, the cat would not have gone into the water; and, if she had, would not less have been drowned.

The *Prospect of Eton College* suggests nothing to Gray
30 which every beholder does not equally think and feel. His supplication to father Thames, to tell him who drives the hoop or tosses the ball, is useless and puerile. Father Thames has no better means of knowing than himself. His epithet *buxom health* is not elegant; he seems not

to understand the word. Gray thought his language more poetical as it was more remote from common use : finding in Dryden *honey redolent of Spring,* an expression that reaches the utmost limits of our language, Gray drove it a little more beyond common apprehension, by making *gales* to be *redolent of joy and youth.*

Of the *Ode on Adversity* the hint was at first taken from ' O Diva, gratum quæ regis Antium ' ; but Gray has excelled his original by the variety of his sentiments and by their moral application. Of this piece, at once poetical and rational, I will not by slight objections violate the dignity.

My process has now brought me to the *wonderful Wonder of Wonders,* the two Sister Odes ; by which, though either vulgar ignorance or common sense at first universally rejected them, many have been since persuaded to think themselves delighted. I am one of those that are willing to be pleased, and therefore would gladly find the meaning of the first stanza of *The Progress of Poetry.*

Gray seems in his rapture to confound the images of *spreading sound* and *running water.* A *stream of music* may be allowed ; but where does *Music,* however *smooth and strong,* after having visited the *verdant vales, rowl down the steep amain,* so as that *rocks and nodding groves rebellow to the roar* ? If this be said of *Music,* it is nonsense ; if it be said of *Water,* it is nothing to the purpose.

The second stanza, exhibiting Mars's car and Jove's eagle, is unworthy of further notice. Criticism disdains to chase a schoolboy to his common-places.

To the third it may likewise be objected that it is drawn from Mythology, though such as may be more easily assimilated to real life. Idalia's *velvet-green* has something of cant. An epithet or metaphor drawn from Nature ennobles Art ; an epithet or metaphor drawn from Art

degrades Nature. Gray is too fond of words arbitrarily
compounded. *Many-twinkling* was formerly censured as
not analogical; we may say *many-spotted*, but scarcely
many-spotting. This stanza, however, has something
pleasing.

Of the second ternary of stanzas, the first endeavours to
tell something, and would have told it had it not been
crossed by Hyperion; the second describes well enough
the universal prevalence of Poetry; but I am afraid that
the conclusion will not rise from the premises. The caverns
of the North and the plains of Chili are not the residences
of *Glory* and *generous Shame*. But that Poetry and Virtue
go always together is an opinion so pleasing that I can
forgive him who resolves to think it true.

The third stanza sounds big with *Delphi*, and *Egean*,
and *Ilissus*, and *Meander*, and *hallowed fountain* and
solemn sound; but in all Gray's odes there is a kind
of cumbrous splendour which we wish away. His position
is at last false: in the time of Dante and Petrarch, from
whom he derives our first school of poetry, Italy was
overrun by *tyrant power* and *coward vice*; nor was our
state much better when we first borrowed the Italian
arts.

Of the third ternary, the first gives a mythological birth
of Shakespeare. What is said of that mighty genius is
true; but it is not said happily: the real effects of this
poetical power are put out of sight by the pomp of
machinery. Where truth is sufficient to fill the mind,
fiction is worse than useless; the counterfeit debases the
genuine.

His account of Milton's blindness, if we suppose it caused
by study in the formation of his poem, a supposition surely
allowable, is poetically true, and happily imagined. But
the *car* of Dryden, with his *two coursers*, has nothing in it

peculiar; it is a car in which any other rider may be placed.

The Bard appears, at the first view, to be, as Algarotti and others have remarked, an imitation of the prophecy of Nereus. Algarotti thinks it superior to its original; and, if preference depends only on the imagery and animation of the two poems, his judgement is right. There is in *The Bard* more force, more thought, and more variety. But to copy is less than to invent, and the copy has been unhappily produced at a wrong time. The fiction of Horace 10 was to the Romans credible; but its revival disgusts us with apparent and unconquerable falsehood. *Incredulus odi.*

To select a singular event, and swell it to a giant's bulk by fabulous appendages of spectres and predictions, has little difficulty, for he that forsakes the probable may always find the marvellous. And it has little use ; we are affected only as we believe ; we are improved only as we find something to be imitated or declined. I do not see that *The Bard* promotes any truth, moral or political. 20

His stanzas are too long, especially his epodes ; the ode is finished before the ear has learned its measures, and consequently before it can receive pleasure from their consonance and recurrence.

Of the first stanza the abrupt beginning has been celebrated ; but technical beauties can give praise only to the inventor. It is in the power of any man to rush abruptly upon his subject, that has read the ballad of *Johnny Armstrong,*

Is there ever a man in all Scotland— 30

The initial resemblances, or alliterations, *ruin, ruthless, helm nor hauberk,* are below the grandeur of a poem that endeavours at sublimity.

In the second stanza the Bard is well described ; but in

the third we have the puerilities of obsolete mythology.
When we are told that *Cadwallo hush'd the stormy main*,
and that *Modred* made *huge Plinlimmon bow his cloud-top'd
head*, attention recoils from the repetition of a tale that,
even when it was first heard, was heard with scorn.

The *weaving* of the *winding sheet* he borrowed, as
he owns, from the northern Bards; but their texture,
however, was very properly the work of female powers, as
the art of spinning the thread of life in another mythology.
10 Theft is always dangerous; Gray has made weavers of his
slaughtered bards, by a fiction outrageous and incongruous.
They are then called upon to *Weave the warp, and weave
the woof*, perhaps with no great propriety; for it is by
crossing the *woof* with the *warp* that men *weave* the *web*
or piece; and the first line was dearly bought by the
admission of its wretched correspondent, *Give ample
room and verge enough*. He has, however, no other line as
bad.

The third stanza of the second ternary is commended,
20 I think, beyond its merit. The personification is indistinct.
Thirst and *Hunger* are not alike, and their features, to
make the imagery perfect, should have been discriminated.
We are told, in the same stanza, how *towers* are *fed*.
But I will no longer look for particular faults; yet let it
be observed that the ode might have been concluded with
an action of better example; but suicide is always to be
had, without expense of thought.

These odes are marked by glittering accumulations of
ungraceful ornaments; they strike, rather than please;
30 the images are magnified by affectation; the language is
laboured into harshness. The mind of the writer seems to
work with unnatural violence. *Double, double, toil and
trouble*. He has a kind of strutting dignity, and is tall
by walking on tiptoe. His art and his struggle are too

visible, and there is too little appearance of ease and nature.

To say that he has no beauties, would be unjust: a man like him, of great learning and great industry, could not but produce something valuable. When he pleases least, it can only be said that a good design was ill directed.

His translations of Northern and Welsh Poetry deserve praise; the imagery is preserved, perhaps often improved; but the language is unlike the language of other poets.

In the character of his *Elegy* I rejoice to concur with the common reader; for by the common sense of readers uncorrupted with literary prejudices, after all the refinements of subtilty and the dogmatism of learning, must be finally decided all claim to poetical honours. The *Church-yard* abounds with images which find a mirror in every mind, and with sentiments to which every bosom returns an echo. The four stanzas beginning *Yet even these bones* are to me original: I have never seen the notions in any other place; yet he that reads them here, persuades himself that he has always felt them. Had Gray written often thus, it had been vain to blame, and useless to praise him.

GOLDSMITH'S

Review of the Pindaric Odes

The Monthly Review, September 1757

As this publication seems designed for those who have formed their taste by the models of antiquity, the generality of readers cannot be supposed adequate judges of its merit ; nor will the poet, it is presumed, be greatly disappointed if he finds them backward in commending a performance not entirely suited to their apprehensions. We cannot, however, without some regret behold those talents so capable of giving pleasure to all, exerted in efforts that, at best, can amuse only the few ; we cannot behold this rising poet seeking fame among the learned, without hinting to him the same advice that Isocrates used to give his scholars, *study the people*. This study it is that has conducted the great masters of antiquity up to immortality. Pindar himself, of whom our modern lyrist is an imitator, appears entirely guided by it. He adapted his works exactly to the dispositions of his countrymen. Irregular, enthusiastic, and quick in transition, he wrote for a people inconstant, of warm imaginations, and exquisite sensibility. He chose the most popular subjects, and all his allusions are to customs well known, in his days, to the meanest person. His English imitator wants those advantages. He speaks to a people not easily impressed with new ideas ; extremely tenacious of the old ; with difficulty warmed ; and as slowly cooling again. How unsuited then to our national character is that species of poetry which rises upon us with unexpected flights ! where we must hastily catch the thought, or it flies from us ; and, in short, where the reader must largely partake of the poet's enthusiasm, in order to taste his beauties.

To carry the parallel a little farther : the Greek poet wrote in a language the most proper that can be imagined for this species of composition ; lofty, harmonious, and never needing rhyme to heighten the numbers. But, for us, several unsuccessful experiments seem to prove that the English cannot have Odes in blank verse ; while, on the other hand, a natural imperfection attends those which are composed in irregular rhymes :—the similar sound often recurring where it is not expected, and not being found where it is, creates no small confusion to the reader,— 10 who, as we have not seldom observed, beginning in all the solemnity of poetic elocution, is, by frequent disappointments of the rhyme, at last obliged to drawl out the uncomplying numbers into disagreeable prose.

It is by no means our design to detract from the merit of our author's present attempt : we would only intimate that an English poet,—one whom the Muse has *marked for her own*, could produce a more luxuriant bloom of flowers, by cultivating such as are natives of the soil, than by endeavouring to force the exotics of another climate : 20 or, to speak without a metaphor, such a genius as Mr. Gray might give greater pleasure, and acquire a larger portion of fame, if, instead of being an imitator, he did justice to his talents, and ventured to be more an original. These two Odes, it must be confessed, breathe much of the spirit of Pindar ; but then they have caught the seeming obscurity, the sudden transition, and hazardous epithet, of his mighty master ; all which, though evidently intended for beauties, will, probably, be regarded as blemishes by the generality of his readers. In short, they are in some measure a repre- 30 sentation of what Pindar now appears to be, though perhaps not what he appeared to the states of Greece, when they rivalled each other in his applause, and when Pan himself was seen dancing to his melody.

JAMES BEATTIE
on ' The Bard '

From *An Essay on Poetry and Music*, 1776

I HAVE heard the finest Ode in the world blamed for the boldness of its figures, and for what the critic was pleased to call obscurity. He had, I suppose, formed his taste upon Anacreon and Waller, whose Odes are indeed very simple, and would have been very absurd if they had not been simple. But let us recollect the circumstances of Anacreon (considered as the speaker of his own poetry), and of Gray's Welsh Bard.

The former warbles his lays, reclining on a bed of flowers,
10 dissolved in tranquillity and indolence, while all his. faculties seem to be engrossed by one or a few pleasurable objects. The latter, just escaped from the massacre of his brethren, under the complicated agitations of grief, revenge, and despair ; and surrounded with the scenery of rocks, mountains, and torrents, stupendous by nature, and now rendered hideous by desolation, imprecates perdition upon the bloody Edward ; and, seized with prophetic enthusiasm, foretells in the most alarming strains, and typifies by the most dreadful images, the
20 disasters that were to overtake his family and descendents. If perspicuity and simplicity be natural in the songs of Anacreon, as they certainly are, a figurative style and desultory composition are no less natural in this inimitable performance of Gray. And if real prophecy must always be so obscure as not to be fully understood till it is accomplished, because otherwise it would interfere with the free agency of man, that poem which imitates the style of prophecy, must also, if natural, be to a certain degree obscure ; not indeed in the images or words, but in the
30 allusions. And it is in the allusions only, not in the words or images (for these are most emphatical and picturesque),

that this poem partakes of obscurity; and even its allusions will hardly seem obscure to those who are acquainted with the history of England. Those critics, therefore, who find fault with this poem, because it is not so simple as the songs of Anacreon, or the love-verses of Shenstone and Waller, may as well blame Shakespeare, because Othello does not speak in the sweet and simple language of Desdemona. Horace has no where attempted a theme of such animation and sublimity as this of Gray; and yet Horace, like his master Pindar, is often bold in his transitions, and in the style of many of his odes extremely figurative. But this we not only excuse but applaud, when we consider that in those odes the assumed character of the speaker is enthusiasm, which in all its operations is somewhat violent, and must therefore give vehemence both to thought and to language.

COWPER ON GRAY

Letter to Joseph Hill, April 1777

MY DEAR FRIEND.—Thanks for a turbot, a lobster, and Captain Brydone; a gentleman who relates his travels so agreeably, that he deserves always to travel with an agreeable companion. I have been reading Gray's works and think him the only poet since Shakespeare entitled to the character of Sublime. Perhaps you will remember that I once had a different opinion of him. I was prejudiced. He did not belong to our Thursday society, and was an Eton man, which lowered him prodigiously in our esteem. I once thought Swift's letters the best that could be written; but I like Gray's better. His humour or his wit or whatever it is to be called is never ill-natured or offensive, and yet I think equally poignant with the Dean's.

I am, Yours affectionately
WM. COWPER.

WORDSWORTH ON GRAY
(a) His Diction

From the Preface to *Lyrical Ballads*, 1800

IF in a poem there should be found a series of lines, or
even a single line, in which the language, though naturally
arranged and according to the strict laws of metre, does not
differ from that of prose, there is a numerous class of
critics who, when they stumble upon these prosaisms as
they call them, imagine that they have made a notable
discovery, and exult over the Poet as over a man ignorant
of his own profession. Now these men would establish
a canon of criticism which the reader will conclude he
10 must utterly reject, if he wishes to be pleased with these
volumes. And it would be a most easy task to prove to
him that not only the language of a large portion of every
good poem, even of the most elevated character, must
necessarily, except with reference to the metre, in no
respect differ from that of good prose, but likewise that
some of the most interesting parts of the best poems will
be found to be strictly the language of prose when prose is
well written. The truth of this assertion might be demon-
strated by innumerable passages from almost all the
20 poetical writings, even of Milton himself. To illustrate
the subject in a general manner, I will here adduce a short
composition of Gray, who was at the head of those who
by their reasonings have attempted to widen the space of
separation betwixt Prose and Metrical composition, and
was more than any other man curiously elaborate in the
structure of his own poetic diction.

> In vain to me the smiling mornings shine,
> And reddening Phœbus lifts his golden fire :
> The birds in vain their amorous descant join,
> 30   Or cheerful fields resume their green attire :

These ears, alas! for other notes repine ;
A different object do these eyes require ;
My lonely anguish melts no heart but mine ;
And in my breast the imperfect joys expire ;
Yet morning smiles the busy race to cheer,
And new-born pleasure brings to happier men ;
The fields to all their wonted tribute bear ;
To warm their little loves the birds complain.
I fruitless mourn to him that cannot hear,
And weep the more because I weep in vain.   10

It will easily be perceived that the only part of this
Sonnet which is of any value is the lines printed in Italics :
it is equally obvious that except in the rhyme, and in the
use of the single word ' fruitless ' for fruitlessly, which is
so far a defect, the language of these lines does in no respect
differ from that of prose.

(b) His Epitaphs

From the third essay *Upon Epitaphs*, written for *The Friend* in 1810,
published 1876

THE latter part of the following by Gray is almost the
only instance among the metrical epitaphs in our language
of the last century, which I remember, of affecting thoughts
rising naturally and keeping themselves pure from vicious   20
diction ; and therefore retaining their appropriate powers
over the mind.

Epitaph on Mrs. Clark.

Lo! where the silent marble weeps,
A friend, a wife, a mother, sleeps ;
A heart, within whose sacred cell
The peaceful virtues loved to dwell.

Affection warm, and love sincere,
And soft humanity were there.
In agony, in death resigned,
She felt the wound she left behind.
Her infant image, here below,
Sits smiling on a father's woe ;
Whom what awaits, while yet he stays
Along the lonely vale of days ?
A pang to secret sorrow dear ;
A sigh, an unavailing tear,
Till time shall every grief remove,
With life, with meaning, and with love.

I have been speaking of faults which are aggravated by
temptations thrown in the way of modern writers when
they compose in metre. The first six lines of this epitaph
are vague and languid, more so than I think would have
been possible had it been written in prose. Yet Gray, who
was so happy in the remaining part, especially the last
four lines, has grievously failed *in prose* upon a subject
which it might have been expected would have bound him
indissolubly to the propriety of Nature and comprehensive
reason. I allude to the conclusion of the epitaph upon his
mother, where he says, ' she was the careful tender mother
of many children, one of whom alone had the misfortune
to survive her '. This is a searching thought, but wholly
out of place. Had it been said of an idiot, of a palsied
child, or of an adult from any cause dependent upon his
mother to a degree of helplessness which nothing but
maternal tenderness and watchfulness could answer, that
he had the misfortune to survive his mother, the thought
would have been just. The same might also have been
wrung from any man (thinking of himself) when his
soul was smitten with compunction or remorse, through
the consciousness of a misdeed from which he might
have been preserved (as he hopes or believes) by his

mother's prudence, by her anxious care if longer continued,
or by the reverential fear of disobeying or offending her.
But even then (unless accompanied with a detail of extraordinary circumstances), if transferred to her monument,
it would have been misplaced, as being too peculiar, and
for reasons which have been before alleged, namely, as
too transitory and poignant. But in an ordinary case,
for a man permanently and conspicuously to record that
this was his fixed feeling ; what is it but to run counter
to the course of nature, which has made it matter of expecta- 10
tion and congratulation that parents should die before
their children ? What is it, if searched to the bottom, but
lurking and sickly selfishness ? Does not the regret include
a wish that the mother should have survived all her
offspring, have witnessed that bitter desolation where
the order of things is disturbed and inverted ? And finally,
does it not withdraw the attention of the Reader from
the subject to the Author of the Memorial, as one to be
commiserated for his strangely unhappy condition, or to
be condemned for the morbid constitution of his feelings, 20
or for his deficiency in judgment ? A fault of the same
kind, though less in degree, is found in the epitaph of Pope
upon Harcourt ; of whom it is said that ' he never gave
his father grief but when he died '. I need not point out
how many situations there are in which such an expression
of feeling would be natural and becoming ; but in a per-
manent inscription things only should be admitted that
have an enduring place in the mind ; and a nice selection
is required even among these.

COLERIDGE

on Gray's Diction

From *Biographia Literaria*, 1817, ch. xviii

IN Mr. Wordsworth's criticism of GRAY's Sonnet, the readers' sympathy with his praise or blame of the different parts is taken for granted rather perhaps too easily. He has not, at least, attempted to win or compel it by argumentative analysis. In *my* conception at least, the lines rejected as of no value do, with the exception of the two first, differ as much and as little from the language of common life, as those which he has printed in italics as possessing genuine excellence. Of the five lines thus honourably distinguished, two of them differ from prose, even more widely than the lines which either precede or follow, in the *position* of the words.

> ' *A different object do these eyes require ;*
> My lonely anguish melts no heart but mine ;
> *And in my breast the imperfect joys expire.*'

But were it otherwise, what would this prove, but a truth, of which no man ever doubted ? Videlicet, that there are sentences, which would be equally in their place both in verse and prose. Assuredly it does not prove the point, which alone requires proof ; namely, that there are not passages, which would suit the one and not suit the other. The first line of this sonnet is distinguished from the ordinary language of men by the epithet to morning. (For we will set aside, at present, the consideration, that the particular word ' *smiling* ' is hackneyed and (as it involves a sort of personification) not quite congruous with the common and material attribute of *shining*.) And, doubtless, this adjunction of epithets for the purpose of additional description, where no particular attention is demanded for the quality of the thing, would be noticed as giving a poetic cast to a man's conversation.   Should the sportsman exclaim, ' *Come boys : the rosy morning calls you up,*' he will be supposed to have some song in his head.   But no one suspects this, when he says, ' A wet morning shall not confine us to our beds.'   This then is either a defect in poetry, or it is not.   Whoever should decide in the *affirmative*, I would request him to re-peruse any one poem of any confessedly great poet from Homer to Milton, or from Æschylus to Shakespeare ; and to strike out (in thought I mean) every instance of this kind.   If the number of these fancied erasures did not startle him ; or if he continued to deem the work improved by their total omission ; he must advance reasons of no ordinary strength and evidence, reasons grounded in the essence of human nature.   Otherwise, I should not hesitate to consider him as a man not so much *proof against* all authority, as *dead to* it.

The second line,

' And reddening Phœbus lifts his golden fire ; '

has indeed almost as many faults as words.   But then it is a bad line, not because the language is distinct from that of prose ; but because it conveys incongruous images, because it confounds the cause and the effect, the real *thing* with the personified *representative* of the thing ; in short, because it differs from the language of GOOD SENSE !   That the ' Phœbus ' is hackneyed, and a school-boy image, is an *accidental* fault, dependent on the age in which the author wrote, and not deduced from the nature of the thing.   That it is part of an exploded mythology, is an objection more deeply grounded.   Yet when the torch of ancient learning was re-kindled, so cheering were its beams, that our eldest poets, cut off by Christianity from all *accredited* machinery,

and deprived of all *acknowledged* guardians and symbols
of the great objects of nature, were naturally induced to
adopt, as a *poetic* language, those fabulous personages, those
forms of the supernatural in nature, which had given them
such dear delight in the poems of their great masters. Nay,
even at this day what scholar of genial taste will not so far
sympathize with them, as to read with pleasure in PETRARCH,
CHAUCER, or SPENCER, what he would perhaps condemn as
puerile in a modern poet ?

HAZLITT'S

Lecture on Gray

From *Lectures on the English Poets*, 1818

10 I SHOULD conceive that Collins had a much greater
poetical genius than Gray: he had more of that fine
madness which is inseparable from it, of its turbid effer-
vescence, of all that pushes it to the verge of agony or
rapture. Gray's Pindaric Odes are, I believe, generally
given up at present : they are stately and pedantic, a kind
of methodical borrowed phrenzy. But I cannot so easily
give up, nor will the world be in any haste to part with
his *Elegy in a Country Church-yard* : it is one of the most
classical productions that ever was penned by a refined and
20 thoughtful mind, moralising on human life. Mr. Coleridge
(in his Literary Life) says, that his friend Mr. Wordsworth
had undertaken to shew that the language of the Elegy
is unintelligible : it has, however, been understood ! The
Ode on a Distant Prospect of Eton College is more mechani-
cal and commonplace ; but it touches on certain strings
about the heart, that vibrate in unison with it to our latest
breath. No one ever passes by Windsor's ' stately heights ',
or sees the distant spires of Eton College below, without

thinking of Gray. He deserves that we should think of him; for he thought of others, and turned a trembling, ever-watchful ear to 'the still sad music of humanity'. His Letters are inimitably fine. If his poems are sometimes finical and pedantic, his prose is quite free from affectation. He pours his thoughts out upon paper as they arise in his mind; and they arise in his mind without pretence, or constraint, from the pure impulse of learned leisure and contemplative indolence. He is not here on stilts or in buckram; but smiles in his easy chair, as he moralises 10 through the loopholes of retreat, on the bustle and raree-show of the world, or on 'those reverend bedlams, colleges and schools'! He had nothing to do but to read and to think, and to tell his friends what he read and thought. His life was a luxurious thoughtful dream. 'Be mine,' he says in one of his Letters, ' to read eternal new romances of Marivaux and Crebillon.' And in another, to shew his contempt for action and the turmoils of ambition, he says to someone, 'Don't you remember Lords —— and ——, who are now great statesmen, little dirty boys playing at 20 cricket ? For my part, I do not feel a bit wiser, or bigger, or older than I did then.'

What an equivalent for not being wise or great, to be always young! What a happiness never to lose or gain anything in the game of human life, by being never any thing more than a looker-on!

CAMPBELL

From *Specimens of the British Poets*, 1819

MR. MATTHIAS, the accomplished editor of Gray, in delineating his poetical character, dwells with peculiar emphasis on the charm of his lyrical versification, which he justly ascribes to the naturally exquisite ear of the poet having been trained to consummate skill in harmony, by long familiarity with the finest models in the most poetical of all languages, the Greek and Italian :

' He was indeed (says Mr. Matthias) the inventor, it may be strictly said so, of a new lyrical metre in his own tongue.
10 The peculiar formation of *his* strophe, antistrophe, and epode, was unknown before him ; and it could only have been planned and perfected by a master genius, who was equally skilled by long and repeated study, and by transfusion into his own mind of the lyric compositions of ancient Greece and of the higher *canzoni* of the Tuscan poets, *di maggior carme e suono*, as it is termed in the commanding energy of their language. Antecedent to *The Progress of Poetry*, and to *The Bard*, no such lyrics had appeared. There is not an ode in the English language which is con-
20 structed like these two compositions ; with such power, such majesty, and such sweetness, with such proportioned pauses and just cadences, with such regulated measures of the verse, with such master principles of lyrical art displayed and exemplified, and, at the same time, with such a concealment of the difficulty, which is lost in the softness and uninterrupted flowing of the lines in each stanza, with such a musical magic, that every verse in it in succession dwells on the ear and harmonizes with that which has gone before.'

30 So far as the versification of Gray is concerned, I have too much pleasure in transcribing these sentiments of Mr. Matthias, to encumber them with any qualifying remarks of my own on that particular subject ; but I

dissent from him in his more general estimate of Gray's genius, when he afterwards speaks of it as ' second to none '.

In order to distinguish the positive merits of Gray from the loftier excellence ascribed to him by his editor, it is unnecessary to resort to the criticisms of Dr. Johnson. Some of them may be just, but their general spirit is malignant and exaggerated. When we look to such beautiful passages in Gray's Odes, as his Indian poet amidst the forests of Chili, or his prophet bard scattering dismay on the array of Edward, and his awe-struck chieftains, on the side of Snowdon—when we regard his elegant taste, not only gathering classical flowers from the Arno and Ilissus, but revealing glimpses of barbaric grandeur amidst the darkness of Runic mythology—when we recollect his ' *thoughts that breathe, and words that burn* ' —his rich personifications, his broad and prominent images, and the crowning charm of his versification, we may safely pronounce that Johnson's critical fulminations have passed over his lyrical character with more noise than destruction.

At the same time it must be recollected, that his beauties are rather crowded into a short compass, than numerous in their absolute sum. The spirit of poetry, it is true, is not to be computed mechanically by tale or measure ; and the abundance of it may enter into a very small bulk of language. But neither language nor poetry is compressible beyond certain limits ; and the poet whose thoughts have been concentrated into a few pages, cannot be expected to have given a very full or interesting image of life in his compositions. A few odes, splendid, spirited, and harmonious, but by no means either faultless or replete with subjects that come home to universal sympathy, and an elegy, unrivalled as it is in that species of composition, these achievements of our poet form, after all, no such extensive grounds of originality, as to entitle their author to be spoken of as in genius 'second to none'. He had not, like Goldsmith, the art of unbending from grace to levity. Nothing can be more unexhilarating than his attempts at wit and humour, either in his letters or lighter poetry. In his graver and better strains some of the most exquisite ideas are his own; and his taste, for the most part, adorned, and skilfully recast, the forms of thought and expression which he borrowed from others. If his works often ' whisper whence they stole their balmy spoils ', it is not from plagiarism, but from a sensibility that sought and selected the finest impressions of genius from other gifted minds. But still there is a higher appearance of culture than fertility, of acquisition than originality in Gray. He is not that being of independent imagination, that native and creative spirit, of whom we should say, that he would have plunged into the flood of poetry had there been none to leap before him. Nor were his learned acquisitions turned to the very highest account. He was the architect of no poetical design of extensive or intricate compass. One noble historical picture, it must be confessed, he has left in the opening scene of his Bard; and the sequel of that ode, though it is not perhaps the most interesting prophecy of English history which we could suppose Inspiration to pronounce, contains many richly poetical conceptions. It is, however, exclusively in the opening of the Bard that Gray can be ever said to have portrayed a grand, distinct, and heroic scene of fiction.

The obscurity so often objected to him is certainly a defect not to be justified by the authority of Pindar, more than anything else that is intrinsically objectionable. But it has been exaggerated. He is nowhere so obscure as not to be intelligible by recurring to the passage. And it may be further observed, that Gray's lyrical obscurity never arises, as in some writers, from undefined ideas or paradoxical sentiments. On the contrary, his moral spirit is as explicit as it is majestic ; and deeply read as he was in Plato, he is never metaphysically perplexed. The fault of his meaning is to be latent, not indefinite or confused. When we give his beauties re-perusal and attention, they kindle and multiply to the view. The thread of association that conducts to his remote allusions, or that connects his abrupt transitions, ceases then to be invisible. His lyrical pieces are like paintings on glass, which must be placed in a strong light to give out the perfect radiance of their colouring. 10

Selections from

GRAY'S

POETRY and LETTERS

ODE on the SPRING.

Lo ! where the rosy-bosom'd Hours,
Fair VENUS' train appear,
Disclose the long-expecting flowers,
And wake the purple year !
The Attic warbler pours her throat,
Responsive to the cuckow's note,
The untaught harmony of spring :
While whisp'ring pleasure as they fly,
Cool Zephyrs thro' the clear blue sky
Their gather'd fragrance fling.   10

Where'er the oak's thick branches stretch
A broader browner shade ;
Where'er the rude and moss-grown beech
O'er-canopies the glade,*
Beside some water's rushy brink
With me the Muse shall sit, and think
(At ease reclin'd in rustic state)
How vain the ardour of the Crowd,
How low, how little are the Proud,
How indigent the Great !   20

Still is the toiling hand of Care :
The panting herds repose :
Yet hark, how thro' the peopled air
The busy murmur glows !

*   —————————a bank
O'ercanopied with luscious woodbine.
Shakesp. Mids. Night's Dream.

The insect youth are on the wing,
Eager to taste the honied spring,
And float amid the liquid noon * :
Some lightly o'er the current skim,
Some shew their gayly-gilded trim
Quick-glancing to the sun.†   30

To Contemplation's sober eye ‡
Such is the race of Man :
And they that creep, and they that fly,
Shall end where they began.
Alike the Busy and the Gay
But flutter thro' life's little day,
In fortune's varying colours drest :
Brush'd by the hand of rough Mischance,
Or chill'd by age, their airy dance
They leave, in dust to rest.   40

Methinks I hear in accents low
The sportive kind reply :
Poor moralist ! and what art thou ?
A solitary fly !
Thy Joys no glittering female meets,
No hive hast thou of hoarded sweets,
No painted plumage to display :
On hasty wings thy youth is flown ;
Thy sun is set, thy spring is gone——
We frolick, while 'tis May.   50

* " Nare per æstatem liquidam——"
                                        Virgil.   Georg. lib. 4.
†   ——sporting with quick glance
   Shew to the sun their waved coats drop'd with gold.
                              Milton's Paradise Lost, book 7.
‡ While insects from the threshold preach, *&c.*
                              M. GREEN, *in the Grotto.*
                         Dodsley's Miscellanies, Vol. V. *p.* 161.

O D E

On the Death of a

F A V O U R I T E   C A T ,

Drowned in a Tub of Gold Fishes.

'TWAS on a lofty vase's side,
Where China's gayest art had dy'd
  The azure flowers, that blow ;
Demurest of the tabby kind,
The pensive Selima reclin'd,
  Gazed on the lake below.

Her conscious tail her joy declar'd ;
The fair round face, the snowy beard,
  The velvet of her paws,
Her coat, that with the tortoise vies,   10
Her ears of jet, and emerald eyes,
  She saw ; and purr'd applause.

Still had she gaz'd ; but 'midst the tide
Two angel forms were seen to glide,
  The Genii of the stream :
Their scaly armour's Tyrian hue
Thro' richest purple to the view
  Betray'd a golden gleam.

The hapless Nymph with wonder saw :
A whisker first and then a claw,   20
  With many an ardent wish,
She stretch'd in vain to reach the prize.
What female heart can gold despise ?
  What Cat's averse to fish ?

Presumptuous Maid ! with looks intent
Again she stretch'd, again she bent,
   Nor knew the gulf between.
(Malignant Fate sat by, and smil'd)
The slipp'ry verge her feet beguil'd,
   She tumbled headlong in.   30

Eight times emerging from the flood
She mew'd to ev'ry watry God,
   Some speedy aid to send.
No Dolphin came, no Nereid stirr'd :
Nor cruel *Tom*, nor *Susan* heard.
   A Fav'rite has no friend !

From hence, ye Beauties, undeceiv'd,
Know, one false step is ne'er retriev'd,
   And be with caution bold.
Not all that tempts your wand'ring eyes   40
And heedless hearts, is lawful prize ;
   Nor all, that glisters, gold.

ODE

On a Distant Prospect of

ETON COLLEGE.

YE distant spires, ye antique towers,
That crown the watry glade,
Where grateful Science still adores
Her HENRY's * holy Shade ;
And ye, that from the stately brow
Of WINDSOR's heights th' expanse below
Of grove, of lawn, of mead survey,
Whose turf, whose shade, whose flowers among

* King HENRY the Sixth, Founder of the College.

Wanders the hoary Thames along
His silver-winding way.   10

 Ah happy hills, ah pleasing shade,
Ah fields belov'd in vain,
Where once my careless childhood stray'd,
A stranger yet to pain !
I feel the gales, that from ye blow,
A momentary bliss bestow,
As waving fresh their gladsome wing,
My weary soul they seem to sooth,
And,* redolent of joy and youth,
To breathe a second spring.   20

 Say, Father THAMES, for thou hast seen
Full many a sprightly race
Disporting on thy margent green
The paths of pleasure trace,
Who foremost now delight to cleave
With pliant arm thy glassy wave ?
The captive linnet which enthrall ?
What idle progeny succeed
To chase the rolling circle's speed,
Or urge the flying ball ?   30

 While some on earnest business bent
Their murm'ring labours ply
'Gainst graver hours, that bring constraint
To sweeten liberty :
Some bold adventurers disdain
The limits of their little reign,
And unknown regions dare descry :
Still as they run they look behind,
They hear a voice in every wind,
And snatch a fearful joy.   40

---

* And bees their honey redolent of spring.
    Dryden's Fable on the Pythag. System.

Gay hope is theirs by fancy fed,
Less pleasing when possest ;
The tear forgot as soon as shed,
The sunshine of the breast :
Theirs buxom health of rosy hue,
Wild wit, invention ever-new,
And lively chear of vigour born ;
The thoughtless day, the easy night,
The spirits pure, the slumbers light,
That fly th' approach of morn.   50

Alas, regardless of their doom,
The little victims play !
No sense have they of ills to come,
Nor care beyond to-day :
Yet see how all around 'em wait
The Ministers of human fate,
And black Misfortune's baleful train !
Ah, shew them where in ambush stand
To seize their prey the murth'rous band !
Ah, tell them, they are men !   60

These shall the fury Passions tear,
The vulturs of the mind,
Disdainful Anger, pallid Fear,
And Shame that sculks behind ;
Or pineing Love shall waste their youth,
Or Jealousy with rankling tooth,
That inly gnaws the secret heart,
And Envy wan, and faded Care,
Grim-visag'd comfortless Despair,
And Sorrow's piercing dart.   70

Ambition this shall tempt to rise,
Then whirl the wretch from high,
To bitter Scorn a sacrifice,
And grinning Infamy.

The stings of Falshood those shall try,
And hard Unkindness' alter'd eye,
That mocks the tear it forc'd to flow ;
And keen Remorse with blood defil'd,
And moody Madness * laughing wild
Amid severest woe.   80

   Lo, in the vale of years beneath
A griesly troop are seen,
The painful family of Death,
More hideous than their Queen :
This racks the joints, this fires the veins,
That every labouring sinew strains,
Those in the deeper vitals rage :
Lo, Poverty, to fill the band,
That numbs the soul with icy hand,
And slow-consuming Age.   90

   To each his suff'rings : all are men,
Condemn'd alike to groan ;
The tender for another's pain,
Th' unfeeling for his own.
Yet ah ! why should they know their fate ?
Since sorrow never comes too late,
And happiness too swiftly flies.
Thought would destroy their paradise.
No more ; where ignorance is bliss,
'Tis folly to be wise.   100

  *   ——Madness laughing in his ireful mood.
              Dryden's Fable of Palamon and Arcite.

HYMN to ADVERSITY.

—Ζῆνα
Τὸν φρονεῖν βροτοὺς ὁδώ-
σαντα, τῷ πάθει μαθὰν
Θέντα κυρίως ἔχειν.

Æschylus, in Agamemnone.

DAUGHTER of JOVE, relentless Power,
Thou Tamer of the human breast,
Whose iron scourge and tort'ring hour,
The Bad affright, afflict the Best !
Bound in thy adamantine chain
The Proud are taught to taste of pain,
And purple Tyrants vainly groan
With pangs unfelt before, unpitied and alone.

When first thy Sire to send on earth
Virtue, his darling Child, design'd,   10
To thee he gave the heav'nly Birth,
And bad to form her infant mind.
Stern rugged Nurse ! thy rigid lore
With patience many a year she bore :
What sorrow was, thou bad'st her know,
And from her own she learn'd to melt at others' woe.

Scared at thy frown terrific, fly
Self-pleasing Folly's idle brood,
Wild Laughter, Noise, and thoughtless Joy,
And leave us leisure to be good.   20
Light they disperse, and with them go
The summer Friend, the flatt'ring Foe ;
By vain Prosperity received,
To her they vow their truth, and are again believed.

Wisdom in sable garb array'd
Immers'd in rapt'rous thought profound,
And Melancholy, silent maid
With leaden eye, that loves the ground,
Still on thy solemn steps attend :
Warm Charity, the gen'ral Friend,   30
With Justice to herself severe,
And Pity, dropping soft the sadly-pleasing tear.

Oh, gently on thy Suppliant's head,
Dread Goddess, lay thy chast'ning hand !
Not in thy Gorgon terrors clad,
Nor circled with the vengeful Band
(As by the Impious thou art seen)
With thund'ring voice, and threat'ning mien,
With screaming Horror's funeral cry,
Despair, and fell Disease, and ghastly Poverty.   40

Thy form benign, oh Goddess, wear,
Thy milder influence impart,
Thy philosophic Train be there
To soften, not to wound my heart.
The gen'rous spark extinct revive,
Teach me to love and to forgive,
Exact my own defects to scan,
What others are, to feel, and know myself a Man.

The PROGRESS of POESY.

A PINDARIC ODE.

Φωνᾶντα συνετοῖσιν· ἐς
Δὲ τὸ πᾶν ἑρμηνέων χατίζει.

Pindar. Olymp. II.

I. 1.

* AWAKE, Æolian lyre, awake,
And give to rapture all thy trembling strings.
From Helicon's harmonious springs
A thousand rills their mazy progress take :
The laughing flowers, that round them blow,
Drink life and fragrance as they flow.
Now the rich stream of music winds along
Deep, majestic, smooth, and strong,
Thro' verdant vales, and Ceres' golden reign :
Now rowling down the steep amain,   10
Headlong, impetuous, see it pour :
The rocks, and nodding groves rebellow to the roar.

I. 2.

† Oh ! Sovereign of the willing soul,
Parent of sweet and solemn-breathing airs,

*　　　Awake, my glory : awake, lute and harp.

David's Psalms.

Pindar styles his own poetry with its musical accompanyments,
Αἰοληὶς μολπή, Αἰολίδες χορδαί, Αἰολίδων πνοαὶ αὐλῶν, Æolian song,
Æolian strings, the breath of the Æolian flute.

The subject and simile, as usual with Pindar, are united. The
various sources of poetry, which gives life and lustre to all it touches,
are here described ; its quiet majestic progress enriching every
subject (otherwise dry and barren) with a pomp of diction and
luxuriant harmony of numbers ; and its more rapid and irresistible
course, when swoln and hurried away by the conflict of tumultuous
passions.

† Power of harmony to calm the turbulent sallies of the soul.
The thoughts are borrowed from the first Pythian of Pindar.

Enchanting shell ! the sullen Cares,
And frantic Passions hear thy soft controul.
On Thracia's hills the Lord of War,
Has curb'd the fury of his car,
And drop'd his thirsty lance at thy command.
* Perching on the scept'red hand   20
Of Jove, thy magic lulls the feather'd king
With ruffled plumes, and flagging wing :
Quench'd in dark clouds of slumber lie
The terror of his beak, and light'nings of his eye.

I. 3.

† Thee the voice, the dance, obey,
Temper'd to thy warbled lay.
O'er Idalia's velvet-green
The rosy-crowned Loves are seen
On Cytherea's day
With antic Sports, and blue-eyed Pleasures,   30
Frisking light in frolic measures ;
Now pursuing, now retreating,
Now in circling troops they meet :
To brisk notes in cadence beating
‡ Glance their many-twinkling feet.
Slow melting strains their Queen's approach declare :
Where'er she turns the Graces homage pay.
With arms sublime, that float upon the air,
In gliding state she wins her easy way :
O'er her warm cheek, and rising bosom, move   40
§ The bloom of young Desire, and purple light of Love.

---

* This is a weak imitation of some incomparable lines in the same Ode.

† Power of harmony to produce all the graces of motion in the body.

‡ Μαρμαρυγὰς θηεῖτο ποδῶν·   θαύμαζε δὲ θυμῷ.   HOMER.   Od. Θ.

§ Λάμπει δ' ἐπὶ πορφυρέῃσι
    Παρείῃσι φῶς ἔρωτος.   PHRYNICHUS, apud Athenæum.

II. 1.

* Man's feeble race what Ills await,
Labour, and Penury, the racks of Pain,
Disease, and Sorrow's weeping train,
And Death, sad refuge from the storms of Fate !
The fond complaint, my Song, disprove,
And justify the laws of Jove.
Say, has he giv'n in vain the heav'nly Muse ?
Night, and all her sickly dews,
Her Spectres wan, and Birds of boding cry,   50
He gives to range the dreary sky :
† Till down the eastern cliffs afar
Hyperion's march they spy, and glitt'ring shafts of war.

II. 2.

‡ In climes beyond the solar § road,
Where shaggy forms o'er ice-built mountains roam,
The Muse has broke the twilight-gloom
To chear the shiv'ring Native's dull abode.
And oft, beneath the od'rous shade
Of Chili's boundless forests laid,
She deigns to hear the savage Youth repeat   60
In loose numbers wildly sweet
Their feather-cinctured Chiefs, and dusky Loves.
Her track, where'er the Goddess roves,
Glory pursue, and generous Shame,
Th' unconquerable Mind, and Freedom's holy flame.

* To compensate the real and imaginary ills of life, the Muse was given to Mankind by the same Providence that sends the Day by its chearful presence to dispel the gloom and terrors of the Night.

†   Or seen the Morning's well-appointed Star
        Come marching up the eastern hills afar.   *Cowley.*

‡ Extensive influence of poetic Genius over the remotest and most uncivilized nations : its connection with liberty, and the virtues that naturally attend on it. [See the Erse, Norwegian, and Welch Fragments, the Lapland and American songs.]

§ " Extra anni solisque vias——"   *Virgil.*
  " Tutta lontana dal camin del sole."   *Petrarch, Canzon 2.*

II. 3.

* Woods, that wave o'er Delphi's steep,
Isles, that crown th' Egæan deep,
Fields, that cool Ilissus laves,
Or where Mæander's amber waves
In lingering Lab'rinths creep,   70
How do your tuneful Echoes languish,
Mute, but to the voice of Anguish ?
Where each old poetic Mountain
Inspiration breath'd around :
Ev'ry shade and hallow'd Fountain
Murmur'd deep a solemn sound :
Till the sad Nine in Greece's evil hour
Left their Parnassus for the Latian plains.
Alike they scorn the pomp of tyrant-Power,
And coward Vice, that revels in her chains.   80
When Latium had her lofty spirit lost,
They sought, oh Albion ! next thy sea-encircled coast.

III. 1.

Far from the sun and summer-gale,
In thy green lap was Nature's † Darling laid,
What time, where lucid Avon stray'd,
To Him the mighty Mother did unveil
Her aweful face : The dauntless Child
Stretch'd forth his little arms, and smiled.
This pencil take (she said) whose colours clear
Richly paint the vernal year :   90

---

* Progress of Poetry from Greece to Italy, and from Italy to
England. Chaucer was not unacquainted with the writings of Dante
or of Petrarch. The Earl of Surrey and Sir Tho. Wyatt had travelled
in Italy, and formed their taste there ; Spenser imitated the Italian
writers ; Milton improved on them : but this School expired soon
after the Restoration, and a new one arose on the French model,
which has subsisted ever since.

† Shakespear.

Thine too these golden keys, immortal Boy !
This can unlock the gates of Joy ;
Of Horrour that, and thrilling Fears,
Or ope the sacred source of sympathetic Tears.

III. 2.

Nor second He *, that rode sublime
Upon the seraph-wings of Extasy,
The secrets of th' Abyss to spy.
† He pass'd the flaming bounds of Place and Time :
‡ The living Throne, the saphire-blaze,
Where Angels tremble, while they gaze,   100
He saw ; but blasted with excess of light,
§ Closed his eyes in endless night.
Behold, where Dryden's less presumptuous car,
Wide o'er the fields of Glory bear
‖ Two Coursers of ethereal race,
¶ With necks in thunder cloath'd, and long-resounding
    pace.

III. 3.

Hark, his hands the lyre explore !
Bright-eyed Fancy hovering o'er
Scatters from her pictured urn
** Thoughts, that breathe, and words, that burn.   110

---

* Milton.
† " ——flammantia mœnia mundi." *Lucretius.*
‡ For the spirit of the living creature was in the wheels—And
above the firmament, that was over their heads, was the likeness
of a throne, as the appearance of a saphire-stone.—This was the
appearance of the glory of the Lord.   *Ezekiel* i. 20, 26, 28.
§ Ὀφθαλμῶν μὲν ἄμερσε· δίδου δ' ἡδεῖαν ἀοιδήν. HOMER. Od.
‖ Meant to express the stately march and sounding energy of
Dryden's rhimes.
¶ Hast thou cloathed his neck with thunder ?   *Job.*
** Words, that weep, and tears, that speak.   *Cowley.*

* But ah ! 'tis heard no more——
Oh ! Lyre divine, what daring Spirit
Wakes thee now ? ho' he inherit
Nor the pride nor ample pinion,
† That the Theban Eagle bear
Sailing with supreme dominion
Thro' the azure deep of air :
Yet oft before his infant eyes would run
Such forms, as glitter in the Muse's ray
With orient hues, unborrow'd of the Sun :   120
Yet shall he mount, and keep his distant way
Beyond the limits of a vulgar fate,
Beneath the Good how far—but far above the Great.

---

* We have had in our language no other odes of the sublime kind,
than that of Dryden on St. Cecilia's day : for Cowley (who had his
merit) yet wanted judgment, style, and harmony, for such a task.
That of Pope is not worthy of so great a man. Mr. Mason indeed
of late days has touched the true chords, and with a masterly hand,
in some of his Choruses,—above all in the last of Caractacus,

> Hark ! heard ye not yon footstep dread ? *&c.*

† Διὸς πρὸς ὄρνιχα θεῖον. Olymp. 2. Pindar compares himself to
that bird, and his enemies to ravens that croak and clamour in vain
below, while it pursues its flight, regardless of their noise.

The BARD.

A PINDARIC ODE.

ADVERTISEMENT.

The following Ode is founded on a Tradition current in
Wales, that EDWARD THE FIRST, when he compleated
the conquest of that country, ordered all the Bards, that
fell into his hands, to be put to death.

I.   1.

'RUIN seize thee, ruthless King!
'Confusion on thy banners wait,
'Tho' fann'd by Conquest's crimson wing
'* They mock the air with idle state.
'Helm, nor † Hauberk's twisted mail,
'Nor even thy virtues, Tyrant, shall avail
'To save thy secret soul from nightly fears,
'From Cambria's curse, from Cambria's tears!'
Such were the sounds, that o'er the ‡ crested pride
Of the first Edward scatter'd wild dismay,   10
As down the steep of § Snowdon's shaggy side
He wound with toilsome march his long array.

---

*   Mocking the air with colours idly spread.
                                   Shakespear's King John.
    † The Hauberk was a texture of steel ringlets, or rings interwoven,
forming a coat of mail, that sate close to the body, and adapted
itself to every motion.
    ‡ ——The crested adder's pride.   *Dryden's Indian Queen.*
    § *Snowdon* was a name given by the Saxons to that mountainous
tract, which the Welch themselves call *Craigian-eryri*: it included
all the highlands of Caernarvonshire and Merionethshire, as far east
as the river Conway. R. Hygden speaking of the castle of Conway
built by King Edward the first, says, 'Ad ortum amnis Conway
'ad clivum montis Erery;' and Matthew of Westminster, (ad ann.
1283,) 'Apud Aberconway ad pedes montis Snowdoniæ fecit erigi
'castrum forte.'

Stout * Glo'ster stood aghast in speechless trance :
To arms ! cried † Mortimer, and couch'd his quiv'ring
    lance.

I. 2.

On a rock, whose haughty brow
Frowns o'er old Conway's foaming flood,
Robed in the sable garb of woe,
With haggard eyes the Poet stood ;
(‡ Loose his beard, and hoary hair
§ Stream'd, like a meteor, to the troubled air)   20
And with a Master's hand, and Prophet's fire,
Struck the deep sorrows of his lyre.
' Hark, how each giant-oak, and desert cave,
' Sighs to the torrent's aweful voice beneath !
' O'er thee, oh King ! their hundred arms they wave,
' Revenge on thee in hoarser murmurs breath ;
' Vocal no more, since Cambria's fatal day,
' To high-born Hoel's harp, or soft Llewellyn's lay.

I. 3.

' Cold is Cadwallo's tongue,
' That hush'd the stormy main :   30
' Brave Urien sleeps upon his craggy bed :
' Mountains, ye mourn in vain
' Modred, whose magic song
' Made huge Plinlimmon bow his cloud-top'd head.

  * Gilbert de Clare, surnamed the Red, Earl of Gloucester and
Hertford, son-in-law to King Edward.
  † Edmond de Mortimer, Lord of Wigmore.
  They both were *Lords-Marchers*, whose lands lay on the borders
of Wales, and probably accompanied the King in this expedition.
  ‡ The image was taken from a well-known picture of Raphaël,
representing the Supreme Being in the vision of Ezekiel : there are
two of these paintings (both believed original), one at Florence, the
other at Paris.
  §   Shone, like a meteor, streaming to the wind.
                                Milton's Paradise Lost.

' * On dreary Arvon's shore they lie,
' Smear'd with gore, and ghastly pale :
' Far, far aloof th' affrighted ravens fail ;
' The famish'd † Eagle screams, and passes by.
' Dear lost companions of my tuneful art,
' ‡ Dear, as the light that visits these sad eyes,   40
' ‡ Dear, as the ruddy drops that warm my heart,
' Ye died amidst your dying country's cries—'
' No more I weep. They do not sleep.
' On yonder cliffs, a griesly band,
' I see them sit, they linger yet,
' Avengers of their native land :
' With me in dreadful harmony † they join,
' And § weave with bloody hands the tissue of thy line.'

II. I.

" Weave the warp, and weave the woof,
" The winding-sheet of Edward's race.   50
" Give ample room, and verge enough
" The characters of hell to trace.
" Mark the year, and mark the night,
" || When Severn shall re-eccho with affright
" The shrieks of death, thro' Berkley's roofs that ring,
" Shrieks of an agonizing King !

* The shores of Caernarvonshire opposite to the isle of Anglesey.
† Cambden and others observe, that eagles used annually to build their aerie among the rocks of Snowdon, which from thence (as some think) were named by the Welch *Craigian-eryri*, or the crags of the eagles. At this day (I am told) the highest point of Snowdon is called *the eagle's nest*. That bird is certainly no stranger to this island, as the Scots, and the people of Cumberland, Westmoreland, &c. can testify : it even has built its nest in the Peak of Derbyshire. [See Willoughby's Ornithol. published by Ray.]
‡ As dear to me as are the ruddy drops,
  That visit my sad heart———   *Shakesp. Jul. Cæsar.*
§ See the Norwegian Ode, that follows.
|| Edward the Second, cruelly butchered in Berkley-Castle.

" * She-Wolf of France, with unrelenting fangs,

" That tear'st the bowels of thy mangled Mate,

" † From thee be born, who o'er thy country hangs

" The scourge of Heav'n. What Terrors round him wait! 60

" Amazement in his van, with Flight combined,

" And Sorrow's faded form, and Solitude behind.

II. 2.

" Mighty Victor, mighty Lord,

" ‡ Low on his funeral couch he lies !

" No pitying heart, no eye, afford

" A tear to grace his obsequies.

" Is the sable § Warriour fled ?

" Thy son is gone. He rests among the Dead.

" The Swarm, that in thy noon-tide beam were born ?

" Gone to salute the rising Morn.   70

" Fair ‖ laughs the Morn, and soft the Zephyr blows,

" While proudly riding o'er the azure realm

" In gallant trim the gilded Vessel goes ;

" Youth on the prow, and Pleasure at the helm ;

" Regardless of the sweeping Whirlwind's sway,

" That, hush'd in grim repose, expects his evening-prey.

II. 3.

" ¶ Fill high the sparkling bowl

" The rich repast prepare,

" Reft of a crown, he yet may share the feast :

---

* Isabel of France, Edward the Second's adulterous Queen.

† Triumphs of Edward the Third in France.

‡ Death of that King, abandoned by his Children, and even robbed in his last moments by his Courtiers and his Mistress.

§ Edward, the Black Prince, dead some time before his Father.

‖ Magnificence of Richard the Second's reign. See Froissard, and other contemporary Writers.

¶ Richard the Second, (as we are told by Archbishop Scroop and the confederate Lords in their manifesto, by Thomas of Walsingham, and all the older Writers,) was starved to death. The story of his assassination by Sir Piers of Exon, is of much later date.

" Close by the regal chair   80
" Fell Thirst and Famine scowl
" A baleful smile upon their baffled Guest.
" Heard ye the din of * battle bray,
" Lance to lance, and horse to horse ?
" Long Years of havock urge their destined course,
" And thro' the kindred squadrons mow their way.
" Ye Towers of Julius †, London's lasting shame,
" With many a foul and midnight murther fed,
" Revere his ‡ Consort's faith, his Father's § fame,
" And spare the meek ‖ Usurper's holy head.   90
" Above, below, the ¶ rose of snow,
" Twined with her blushing foe, we spread :
" The bristled ** Boar in infant-gore
" Wallows beneath the thorny shade.
" Now, Brothers, bending o'er th' accursed loom
" Stamp we our vengeance deep, and ratify his doom.

III. 1.

" Edward, lo ! to sudden fate
" (Weave we the woof. The thread is spun
" †† Half of thy heart we consecrate.
" (The web is wove. The work is done.) "   100

* Ruinous civil wars of York and Lancaster.

† Henry the Sixth, George Duke of Clarence, Edward the Fifth, Richard Duke of York, &c. believed to be murthered secretly in the Tower of London. The oldest part of that structure is vulgarly attributed to Julius Cæsar.

‡ Margaret of Anjou, a woman of heroic spirit, who struggled hard to save her Husband and her Crown.

§ Henry the Fifth.

‖ Henry the Sixth very near being canonized. The line of Lancaster had no right of inheritance to the Crown.

¶ The white and red roses, devices of York and Lancaster.

** The silver Boar was the badge of Richard the Third ; whence he was usually known in his own time by the name of *the Boar*.

†† Eleanor of Castile died a few years after the conquest of Wales. The heroic proof she gave of her affection for her Lord is well known.

'Stay, oh stay! nor thus forlorn
'Leave me unbless'd, unpitied, here to mourn :
'In yon bright track, that fires the western skies,
'They melt, they vanish from my eyes.
'But oh! what solemn scenes on Snowdon's height
'Descending slow their glitt'ring skirts unroll?
'Visions of glory, spare my aching sight,
'Ye unborn Ages, crowd not on my soul!
'No more our long-lost * Arthur we bewail.   109
'All-hail, † ye genuine Kings, Britannia's Issue, hail!

III. 2.

'Girt with many a Baron bold
'Sublime their starry fronts they rear ;
'And gorgeous Dames, and Statesmen old
'In bearded majesty, appear.
'In the midst a Form divine!
'Her eye proclaims her of the Briton-Line ;
'Her lyon-port ‡, her awe-commanding face,
'Attemper'd sweet to virgin-grace.
'What strings symphonious tremble in the air,
'What strains of vocal transport round her play!   120

The monuments of his regret, and sorrow for the loss of her, are still to be seen at Northampton, Geddington, Waltham, and other places.

* It was the common belief of the Welch nation, that King Arthur was still alive in Fairy-Land, and should return again to reign over Britain.

† Both Merlin and Taliessin had prophesied, that the Welch should regain their sovereignty over this island ; which seemed to be accomplished in the House of Tudor.

‡ Speed relating an audience given by Queen Elizabeth to Paul Dzialinski, Ambassadour of Poland, says, ' And thus she, lion-like 'rising, daunted the malapert Orator no less with her stately port 'and majestical deporture, than with the tartnesse of her princelie 'checkes.'

' Hear from the grave, great Taliessin *, hear ;
' They breathe a soul to animate thy clay.
' Bright Rapture calls, and soaring, as she sings,
' Waves in the eye of Heav'n her many-colour'd wings.

III. 3.

' The verse adorn again
' † Fierce War, and faithful Love,
' And Truth severe, by fairy Fiction drest.
' In ‡ buskin'd measures move
' Pale Grief, and pleasing Pain,
' With Horrour, Tyrant of the throbbing breast.   130
' A § Voice, as of the Cherub-Choir,
' Gales from blooming Eden bear ;
' || And distant warblings lessen on my ear,
' That lost in long futurity expire.
' Fond impious Man, think'st thou, yon sanguine cloud,
' Rais'd by thy breath, has quench'd the Orb of day ?
' To-morrow he repairs the golden flood,
' And warms the nations with redoubled ray.
' Enough for me : With joy I see
' The different doom our Fates assign.   140
' Be thine Despair, and scept'red Care,
' To triumph, and to die, are mine.'
He spoke, and headlong from the mountain's height
Deep in the roaring tide he plung'd to endless night.

---

* Taliessin, Chief of the Bards, flourished in the VIth Century.
His works are still preserved, and his memory held in high venera-
tion among his Countrymen.

† Fierce wars and faithful loves shall moralize my song.
Spenser's Proëme to the Fairy Queen.

‡ Shakespear.
§ Milton.
|| The succession of Poets after Milton's time.

The FATAL SISTERS

AN ODE.

PREFACE.

In the Eleventh Century *Sigurd*, Earl of the Orkney-Islands, went with a fleet of ships and a considerable body of troops into Ireland, to the assistance of *Sictryg with the silken beard*, who was then making war on his father-in-law *Brian*, King of Dublin : the Earl and all his forces were cut to pieces, and *Sictryg* was in danger of a total defeat ; but the enemy had a greater loss by the death of *Brian*, their King, who fell in the action. On Christmas-day, (the day of the battle,) a Native of *Caithness* in Scotland saw at a distance a number of persons on horse-back riding full speed towards a hill, and seeming to enter into it. Curiosity led him to follow them, till looking through an opening in the rocks he saw twelve gigantic figures resembling women : they were all employed about a loom ; and as they wove, they sung the following dreadful Song ; which when they had finished, they tore the web into twelve pieces, and (each taking her portion) galloped Six to the North and as many to the South.

> Now the storm begins to lower,
> (Haste, the loom of Hell prepare,)
> * Iron-sleet of arrowy shower
> † Hurtles in the darken'd air.

Note—The *Valkyriur* were female Divinities, Servants of *Odin* (or *Woden*) in the Gothic mythology. Their name signifies *Chusers of the slain*. They were mounted on swift horses, with drawn swords in their hands ; and in the throng of battle selected such as were destined to slaughter, and conducted them to *Valhalla*, the hall of *Odin*, or paradise of the Brave ; where they attended the banquet, and served the departed Heroes with horns of mead and ale.

* How quick they wheel'd ; and flying, behind them shot
  Sharp sleet of arrowy shower—— *Milton's Paradise Regained.*
† The noise of battle hurtled in the air. *Shakesp. Jul. Cæsar.*

Glitt'ring lances are the loom,
Where the dusky warp we strain,
Weaving many a Soldier's doom,
Orkney's woe, and *Randver*'s bane.

See the griesly texture grow,
('Tis of human entrails made,)   10
And the weights, that play below,
Each a gasping Warriour's head.

Shafts for shuttles, dipt in gore,
Shoot the trembling cords along.
Sword, that once a Monarch bore,
Keep the tissue close and strong.

Mista black, terrific Maid,
Sangrida, and *Hilda* see,
Join the wayward work to aid :
'Tis the woof of victory.   20

Ere the ruddy sun be set,
Pikes must shiver, javelins sing,
Blade with clattering buckler meet,
Hauberk crash, and helmet ring.

(Weave the crimson web of war)
Let us go, and let us fly,
Where our Friends the conflict share,
Where they triumph, where they die.

As the paths of fate we tread,
Wading thro' th' ensanguin'd field :   30
Gondula, and *Geira*, spread
O'er the youthful King your shield.

We the reins to slaughter give,
Ours to kill, and ours to spare :
Spite of danger he shall live.
(Weave the crimson web of war.)

They, whom once the desart-beach
Pent within its bleak domain,
Soon their ample sway shall stretch
O'er the plenty of the plain.   40

Low the dauntless Earl is laid,
Gor'd with many a gaping wound :
Fate demands a nobler head ;
Soon a King shall bite the ground.

Long his loss shall Eirin weep,
Ne'er again his likeness seè ;
Long her strains in sorrow steep,
Strains of Immortality !

Horror covers all the heath,
Clouds of carnage blot the sun.   50
Sisters, weave the web of death ;
Sisters, cease, the work is done.

Hail the task, and hail the hands !
Songs of joy and triumph sing !
Joy to the victorious bands ;
Triumph to the younger King.

Mortal, thou that hear'st the tale,
Learn the tenour of our song.
Scotland, thro' each winding vale
Far and wide the notes prolong.   60

Sisters, hence with spurs of speed :
Each her thundering faulchion wield ;
Each bestride her sable steed.
Hurry, hurry to the field.

The DESCENT of ODIN.

AN ODE.

UPROSE the King of Men with speed,
And saddled strait his coal-black steed ;
Down the yawning steep he rode,
That leads to * HELA's drear abode.
Him the Dog of Darkness spied,
His shaggy throat he open'd wide,
While from his jaws, with carnage fill'd,
Foam and human gore distill'd :
Hoarse he bays with hideous din,
Eyes that glow, and fangs, that grin ;   10
And long pursues, with fruitless yell,
The Father of the powerful spell.
Onward still his way he takes,
(The groaning earth beneath him shakes,)
Till full before his fearless eyes
The portals nine of hell arise.

Right against the eastern gate,
By the moss-grown pile he sate ;
Where long of yore to sleep was laid
The dust of the prophetic Maid.   20
Facing to the northern clime,
Thrice he traced the runic rhyme ;
Thrice pronounc'd, in accents dread,
The thrilling verse that wakes the Dead ;
Till from out the hollow ground
Slowly breath'd a sullen sound.

* *Niflheimr*, the hell of the Gothic nations, consisted of nine worlds, to which were devoted all such as died of sickness, old-age, or by any other means than in battle : Over it presided HELA, the Goddess of Death.

PR.   What call unknown, what charms presume
To break the quiet of the tomb ?
Who thus afflicts my troubled sprite,
And drags me from the realms of night ?   30
Long on these mould'ring bones have beat
The winter's snow, the summer's heat,
The drenching dews, and driving rain !
Let me, let me sleep again.
Who is he,. with voice unblest,
That calls me from the bed of rest ?

O.   A Traveller, to thee unknown,
Is he that calls, a Warriour's Son.
Thou the deeds of light shalt know ;
Tell me what is done below,   40
For whom yon glitt'ring board is spread,
Drest for whom yon golden bed.

PR.   Mantling in the goblet see
The pure bev'rage of the bee,
O'er it hangs the shield of gold ;
'Tis the drink of *Balder* bold :
Balder's head to death is giv'n.
Pain can reach the Sons of Heav'n !
Unwilling I my lips unclose :
Leave me, leave me to repose.   50

O.   Once again my call obey.
Prophetess, arise, and say,
What dangers *Odin*'s Child await,
Who the Author of his fate.

PR.   In *Hoder's* hand the Heroe's doom :
His Brother sends him to the tomb.
Now my weary lips I close :
Leave me, leave me to repose.

O. Prophetess, my spell obey,
Once again arise, and say,   60
Who th' Avenger of his guilt,
By whom shall *Hoder*'s blood be spilt.

Pr. In the caverns of the west,
By *Odin*'s fierce embrace comprest,
A wond'rous Boy shall *Rinda* bear,
Who ne'er shall comb his raven-hair,
Nor wash his visage in the stream,
Nor see the sun's departing beam ;
Till he on *Hoder's* corse shall smile
Flaming on the fun'ral pile.   70
Now my weary lips I close :
Leave me, leave me to repose.

O. Yet a while my call obey.
Prophetess, awake, and say,
What Virgins these, in speechless woe,
That bend to earth their solemn brow,
That their flaxen tresses tear,
And snowy veils, that float in air.
Tell me whence their sorrows rose :
Then I leave thee to repose.   80

Pr. Ha ! no Traveller art thou,
King of Men, I know thee now,
Mightiest of a mighty line——

O. No boding Maid of skill divine
Art thou, nor Prophetess of good ;
But Mother of the giant-brood !

Pr. Hie thee hence, and boast at home,
That never shall Enquirer come
To break my iron-sleep again ;
Till * *Lok* has burst his tenfold chain.   90

* *Lok* is the evil Being, who continues in chains till the *Twilight of the Gods* approaches, when he shall break his bonds ; the human

Never, till substantial Night
Has reassum'd her ancient right ;
Till wrap'd in flames, in ruin hurl'd,
Sinks the fabric of the world.

The TRIUMPHS of OWEN.

A FRAGMENT.

ADVERTISEMENT.

OWEN succeeded his Father GRIFFIN in the Principality of
NORTH-WALES, A. D. 1120. This battle was fought near
forty Years afterwards.

Owen's praise demands my song,
Owen swift, and Owen strong ;
Fairest flower of Roderic's stem,
* Gwyneth's shield, and Britain's gem
He nor heaps his brooded stores,
Nor on all profusely pours ;
Lord of every regal art,
Liberal hand, and open heart.

Big with hosts of mighty name,
Squadrons three against him came ;   10
This the force of Eirin hiding,
Side by side as proudly riding,
On her shadow long and gay
† Lochlin plows the watry way ;

race, the stars, and sun, shall disappear ; the earth sink in the seas,
and fire consume the skies : even Odin himself and his kindred-
deities shall perish. For a farther explanation of this mythology,
see Mallet's Introduction to the History of Denmark, 1755, Quarto.

   * North-Wales.
   † Denmark.

There the Norman sails afar
Catch the winds, and join the war :
Black and huge along they sweep,
Burthens of the angry deep.

Dauntless on his native sands
* The Dragon-Son of Mona stands ;   20
In glitt'ring arms and glory drest,
High he rears his ruby crest.
There the thund'ring strokes begin,
There the press, and there the din ;
Talymalfra's rocky shore
Echoing to the battle's roar.
Where his glowing eye-balls turn,
Thousand Banners round him burn.

Where he points his purple spear,
Hasty, hasty Rout is there,   30
Marking with indignant eye
Fear to stop, and shame to fly
There Confusion, Terror's child,
Conflict fierce, and Ruin wild,
Agony, that pants for breath,
Despair and honourable Death.

.   .   .

* The red Dragon is the device of Cadwallader, which all his
descendants bore on their banners.

ELEGY

WRITTEN IN A

COUNTRY CHURCH-YARD.

THE Curfew tolls * the knell of parting day,
The lowing herd wind slowly o'er the lea,
The plowman homeward plods his weary way,
And leaves the world to darkness and to me.

Now fades the glimmering landscape on the sight,
And all the air a solemn stillness holds,
Save where the beetle wheels his droning flight,
And drowsy tinklings lull the distant folds;

Save from that yonder ivy-mantled tow'r
The mopeing owl does to the moon complain   10
Of such, as wand'ring near her secret bow'r,
Molest her ancient solitary reign.

Beneath those rugged elms, that yew-tree's shade,
Where heaves the turf in many a mould'ring heap,
Each in his narrow cell for ever laid,
The rude Forefathers of the hamlet sleep.

The breezy call of incense-breathing Morn,
The swallow twitt'ring from the straw-built shed,
The cock's shrill clarion, or the echoing horn,
No more shall rouse them from their lowly bed.   20

For them no more the blazing hearth shall burn,
Or busy housewife ply her evening care :
No children run to lisp their sire's return,
Or climb his knees the envied kiss to share.

*————squilla di lontano,
Che paia 'l giorno pianger, che si muore.
                    Dante. Purgat. [Canto] 8.

Oft did the harvest to their sickle yield,
Their furrow oft the stubborn glebe has broke ;
How jocund did they drive their team afield !
How bow'd the woods beneath their sturdy stroke !

Let not Ambition mock their useful toil,
Their homely joys, and destiny obscure ;   30
Nor Grandeur hear with a disdainful smile,
The short and simple annals of the poor.

The boast of heraldry, the pomp of pow'r,
And all that beauty, all that wealth e'er gave,
Awaits alike th' inevitable hour.
The paths of glory lead but to the grave.

Nor you, ye Proud, impute to These the fault,
If Mem'ry o'er their Tomb no Trophies raise,
Where thro' the long-drawn isle and fretted vault
The pealing anthem swells the note of praise.   40

Can storied urn or animated bust
Back to its mansion call the fleeting breath ?
Can Honour's voice provoke the silent dust,
Or Flatt'ry sooth the dull cold ear of Death ?

Perhaps in this neglected spot is laid
Some heart once pregnant with celestial fire ;
Hands, that the rod of empire might have sway'd,
Or wak'd to extasy the living lyre.

But Knowledge to their eyes her ample page
Rich with the spoils of time did ne'er unroll ;   50
Chill Penury repress'd their noble rage,
And froze the genial current of the soul.

Full many a gem of purest ray serene,
The dark unfathom'd caves of ocean bear :
Full many a flower is born to blush unseen,
And waste its sweetness on the desert air.

Some village-Hampden, that with dauntless breast
The little Tyrant of his fields withstood ;
Some mute inglorious Milton here may rest,
Some Cromwell guiltless of his country's blood.   60

Th' applause of list'ning senates to command,
The threats of pain and ruin to despise,
To scatter plenty o'er a smiling land,
And read their hist'ry in a nation's eyes,

Their lot forbad : nor circumscrib'd alone
Their growing virtues, but their crimes confin'd ;
Forbad to wade through slaughter to a throne,
And shut the gates of mercy on mankind,

The struggling pangs of conscious truth to hide,
To quench the blushes of ingenuous shame,   70
Or heap the shrine of Luxury and Pride
With incense kindled at the Muse's flame.

Far from the madding crowd's ignoble strife,
Their sober wishes never learn'd to stray ;
Along the cool sequester'd vale of life
They kept the noiseless tenor of their way.

Yet ev'n these bones from insult to protect
Some frail memorial still erected nigh,
With uncouth rhimes and shapeless sculpture deck'd,
Implores the passing tribute of a sigh.   80

Their name, their years, spelt by th' unletter'd muse,
The place of fame and elegy supply :
And many a holy text around she strews,
That teach the rustic moralist to die.

For who to dumb Forgetfulness a prey,
This pleasing anxious being e'er resign'd,
Left the warm precincts of the chearful day,
Nor cast one longing ling'ring look behind ?

On some fond breast the parting soul relies,
Some pious drops the closing eye requires ;   90
Ev'n from the tomb the voice of Nature cries,
* Ev'n in our Ashes live their wonted Fires.

For thee, who mindful of th' unhonour'd Dead
Dost in these lines their artless tale relate ;
If chance, by lonely contemplation led,
Some kindred Spirit shall inquire thy fate,

Haply some hoary-headed Swain may say,
' Oft have we seen him at the peep of dawn
' Brushing with hasty steps the dews away
' To meet the sun upon the upland lawn.   100

' There at the foot of yonder nodding beech
' That wreathes its old fantastic roots so high,
' His listless length at noontide would he stretch,
' And pore upon the brook that babbles by.

' Hard by yon wood, now smiling as in scorn,
' Mutt'ring his wayward fancies he would rove,
' Now drooping, woeful wan, like one forlorn,
' Or craz'd with care, or cross'd in hopeless love.

' One morn I miss'd him on the custom'd hill,
' Along the heath and near his fav'rite tree ;   110
' Another came ; nor yet beside the rill,
' Nor up·the lawn, nor at the wood was he ;

' The next with dirges due in sad array
' Slow thro' the church-way path we saw him born.
' Approach and read (for thou can'st read) the lay,
' Grav'd on the stone beneath yon aged thorn.'

> * Ch'i veggio nel pensier, dolce mio fuoco,
>   Fredda una lingua, & due begli occhi chiusi
>   Rimaner doppo noi pien di faville.
>
> *Petrarch. Son.* 169.

The EPITAPH.

Here rests his head upon the lap of Earth
A Youth to Fortune and to Fame unknown.
Fair Science frown'd not on his humble birth,
And Melancholy mark'd him for her own.   120

Large was his bounty, and his soul sincere,
Heav'n did a recompence as largely send :
He gave to Mis'ry all he had, a tear,
He gain'd from Heav'n ('twas all he wish'd) a friend.

No farther seek his merits to disclose,
Or draw his frailties from their dread abode,
(* There they alike in trembling hope repose,)
The bosom of his Father and his God.

ODE on the PLEASURE ARISING
FROM VICISSITUDE.

A FRAGMENT.

Now the golden Morn aloft
  Waves her dew-bespangled wing ;
With vermeil cheek and whisper soft
  She woo's the tardy spring :
Till April starts, and calls around
The sleeping fragrance from the ground ;
And lightly o'er the living scene
Scatters his freshest, tenderest green.

New-born flocks in rustic dance
  Frisking ply their feeble feet.   10
Forgetful of their wintry trance
  The Birds his presence greet.

   * ——paventosa speme.   *Petrarch. Son.* 114.

But chief the Sky-lark warbles high
His trembling thrilling ecstasy
And, less'ning from the dazzled sight,
Melts into air and liquid light.

[Rise, my soul ! on wings of fire,
  Rise the rapturous choir among ;
Hark ! 'tis nature strikes the lyre,
  And leads the general song :]   **20**

Yesterday the sullen year
  Saw the snowy whirlwind fly ;
Mute was the musick of the air,
  The Herd stood drooping by :

Their raptures now that wildly flow,
No yesterday, nor morrow know ;
'Tis Man alone that Joy descries
With forward, and reverted eyes.

Smiles on past Misfortune's brow
  Soft Reflection's hand can trace ;   **30**
And o'er the cheek of Sorrow throw
  A melancholy grace ;
While Hope prolongs our happier hour,
Or deepest shades, that dimly lour
And blacken round our weary way,
Gilds with a gleam of distant day.

Still, where rosy Pleasure leads,
  See a kindred Grief pursue ;
Behind the steps that Misery treads,
  Approaching Comfort view :   **40**
The hues of Bliss more brightly glow,
Chastised by sabler tints of woe ;
And blended form, with artful strife,
The strength and harmony of Life.

See the Wretch, that long has tost
   On the thorny bed of Pain,
At length repair his vigour lost,
   And breathe and walk again :
The meanest flowret of the vale,
The simplest note that swells the gale,   50
The common Sun, the air, and skies,
To him are opening Paradise.

   *   *   *

SKETCH of his OWN CHARACTER.

WRITTEN IN 1761, AND FOUND IN ONE OF HIS POCKET-BOOKS.

Too poor for a bribe, and too proud to importune,
He had not the method of making a fortune :
Could love, and could hate, so was thought somewhat odd ;
No very great wit, he believed in a God :
A place or a pension he did not desire,
But left church and state to Charles Townshend and Squire.

I

To Mr. West.

WHEN you have seen one of my days, you have seen a whole year of my life ; they go round and round like the blind horse in the mill, only he has the satisfaction of fancying he makes a progress and gets some ground ; my eyes are open enough to see the same dull prospect, and to know that having made four-and-twenty steps more, I shall be just where I was ; I may, better than most people, say my life is but a span, were I not afraid lest you should not believe that a person so short-lived could write even so long a letter as this ; in short, I believe I must not send you the history of my own time, till I can send you that also of the reformation. However, as the most undeserving people in the world must sure have the vanity to wish somebody had a regard for them, so I need not wonder at my own, in being pleased that you care about me. You need not doubt, therefore, of having a first row in the front box of my little heart, and I believe you are not in danger of being crowded there ; it is asking you to an old play, indeed, but you will be candid enough to excuse the whole piece for the sake of a few tolerable lines.

For this little while past I have been playing with Statius ; we yesterday had a game at quoits together ; you will easily forgive me for having broke his head, as you have a little pique to him. I send you my translation which I did not engage in because I liked that part of the Poem, nor do I now send it to you because I think it deserves it, but merely to shew you how I mispend my days.

*   *   *   *   *   *

Cambridge, May 8, 1736.

II.

To Mr. West.

You must know that I do not take degrees, and, after this term, shall have nothing more of College impertinencies to undergo, which I trust will be some pleasure to you, as it is a great one to me. I have endured lectures daily and hourly since I came last, supported by the hopes of being shortly at full liberty to give myself up to my friends and classical companions, who, poor souls ! though I see them fallen into great contempt with most people here, yet I cannot help sticking to them, and out of a spirit 10 of obstinacy (I think) love them the better for it ; and indeed, what can I do else ? Must I plunge into metaphysics ? Alas, I cannot see in the dark ; nature has not furnished me with the optics of a cat. Must I pore upon mathematics ? Alas, I cannot see in too much light ; I am no eagle. It is very possible that two and two make four, but I would not give four farthings to demonstrate this ever so clearly ; and if these be the profits of life, give me the amusements of it. The people I behold all around me, it seems, know all this and more, and yet I do 20 not know one of them who inspires me with any ambition of being like him. Surely it was of this place, now Cambridge, but formerly known by the name of Babylon, that the prophet spoke when he said, " the wild beasts of the " desert shall dwell there, and their houses shall be full " of doleful creatures, and owls shall build there, and satyrs " shall dance there ; their forts and towers shall be a den " for ever, a joy of wild asses ; there shall the great owl " make her nest, and lay and hatch and gather under her " shadow ; it shall be a court of dragons ; the screech 30 " owl also shall rest there, and find for herself a place of " rest." You see here is a pretty collection of desolate animals, which is verified in this town to a tittle, and perhaps it may also allude to your habitation, for you know all types may be taken by abundance of handles ; however, I defy your owls to match mine.

If the default of your spirits and nerves be nothing but the effect of the hyp, I have no more to say. We all must submit to that wayward Queen ; I too in no small degree own her sway,

> I feel her influence while I speak her power.

But if it be a real distemper, pray take more care of your health, if not for your own at least for our sakes, and do not be so soon weary of this little world : I do not know what refined friendships you may have contracted in the other, but pray do not be in a hurry to see your acquaintance above ; among your terrestrial familiars, however, though I say it that should not say it, there positively is not one that has a greater esteem for you than

> Yours most sincerely, &c.

Peterhouse, Dec. 1736.

III.

To Mr. West.

After a month's expectation of you, and a fortnight's despair, at Cambridge, I am come to town, and to better hopes of seeing you. If what you sent me last be the product of your melancholy, what may I not expect from your more cheerful hours ? For by this time the ill health that you complain of is (I hope) quite departed ; though, if I were self-interested, I ought to wish for the continuance of any thing that could be the occasion of so much pleasure to me. Low spirits are my true and faithful companions ; they get up with me, go to bed with me, make journeys

and returns as I do ; nay, and pay visits, and will even affect to be jocose, and force a feeble laugh with me ; but most commonly we sit alone together, and are the prettiest insipid company in the world. However, when you come, I believe they must undergo the fate of all humble companions, and be discarded. Would I could turn them to the same use that you have done, and make an Apollo of them. If they could write such verses with me, not hartshorn, nor spirit of amber, nor all that furnishes the
10 closet of an apothecary's widow, should persuade me to part with them : But, while I write to you, I hear the bad news of Lady Walpole's death on Saturday night last. Forgive me if the thought of what my poor Horace must feel on that account, obliges me to have done in reminding you that I am

Yours, &c.

London, Aug. 22, 1737.

IV.

To Mr. Walpole.

I was hindered in my last, and so could not give you all the trouble I would have done. The description of a road, which your coach wheels have so often honoured, it would be needless to give you ; suffice it that I arrived safe at
20 my uncle's, who is a great hunter in imagination ; his dogs take up every chair in the house, so I am forced to stand at this present writing ; and though the gout forbids him galloping after them in the field, yet he continues still to regale his ears and nose with their comfortable noise and stink. He holds me mighty cheap, I perceive, for walking when I should ride, and reading when I should hunt. My comfort amidst all this is, that I have at the distance of half a mile, through a green lane, a forest (the

vulgar call it a common) all my own, at least as good as so, for I spy no human thing in it but myself. It is a little chaos of mountains and precipices ; mountains, it is true, that do not ascend much above the clouds, nor are the declivities quite so amazing as Dover cliff ; but just such hills as people who love their necks as well as I do may venture to climb, and craggs that give the eye as much pleasure as if they were more dangerous : Both vale and hill are covered with most venerable beeches, and other very reverend vegetables, that, like most other ancient people, are always dreaming out their old stories to the winds,

And as they bow their hoary tops relate,
In murm'ring sounds, the dark decrees of fate;
While visions, as poetic eyes avow,
Cling to each leaf and swarm on every bough.

At the foot of one of these squats me I, (*il penseroso*) and there grow to the trunk for a whole morning. The timorous hare and sportive squirrel gambol around me like Adam in Paradise, before he had an Eve ; but I think he did not use to read Virgil, as I commonly do there. In this situation I often converse with my Horace, aloud too, that is talk to you, but I do not remember that I ever heard you answer me. I beg pardon for taking all the conversation to myself, but it is entirely your own fault. We have old Mr. Southern at a Gentleman's house a little way off, who often comes to see us ; he is now seventy-seven years old, and has almost wholly lost his memory ; but is as agreeable as an old man can be, at least I persuade myself so when I look at him, and think of Isabella and Oroonoko. I shall be in Town in about three weeks. Adieu.

September, 1737.

V

To Mr. Walpole.

I sympathize with you in the sufferings which you foresee are coming upon you. We are both at present, I imagine, in no very agreeable situation ; for my part I am under the misfortune of having nothing to do, but it is a misfortune which, thank my stars, I can pretty well bear. You are in a confusion of wine, and roaring, and hunting, and tobacco, and, heaven be praised, you too can pretty well bear it ; while our evils are no more I believe we shall not much repine. I imagine, however, you will
10 rather choose to converse with the living dead, that adorn the walls of your apartments, than with the dead living that deck the middles of them ; and prefer a picture of still life to the realities of a noisy one, and as I guess, will imitate what you prefer, and for an hour or two at noon will stick yourself up as formal as if you had been fixed in your frame for these hundred years, with a pink or rose in one hand, and a great seal ring on the other. Your name, I assure you, has been propagated in these countries by a convert of yours, one * *, he has brought over his
20 whole family to you ; they were before pretty good Whigs, but now they are absolute Walpolians. We have hardly any body in the parish but knows exactly the dimensions of the hall and saloon at Houghton, and begin to believe that the lanthorn is not so great a consumer of the fat of the land as disaffected persons have said : For your reputation, we keep to ourselves your not hunting nor drinking hogan, either of which here would be sufficient to lay your honour in the dust. To-morrow se'nnight I hope to be in Town, and not long after at Cambridge.

I am, &c.

Burnham, Sept. 1737.

VI.

To his Mother.

Rheims, June 21, N. S. 1739.

WE have now been settled almost three weeks in this
city, which is more considerable upon account of its size
and antiquity, than from the number of its inhabitants,
or any advantages of commerce. There is little in it worth
a stranger's curiosity, besides the cathedral church, which
is a vast Gothic building of a surprizing beauty and light-
ness, all covered over with a profusion of little statues,
and other ornaments. It is here the Kings of France are
crowned by the Archbishop of Rheims, who is the first
Peer, and the Primate of the kingdom : The holy vessel 10
made use of on that occasion, which contains the oil, is
kept in the church of St. Nicasius hard by, and is believed
to have been brought by an angel from heaven at the
coronation of Clovis, the first christian king. The streets
in general have but a melancholy aspect, the houses all
old ; the public walks run along the side of a great moat
under the ramparts, where one hears a continual croaking
of frogs ; the country round about is one great plain covered
with vines, which at this time of the year afford no very
pleasing prospect, as being not above a foot high. What 20
pleasures the place denies to the sight, it makes up to the
palate ; since you have nothing to drink but the best
champaigne in the world, and all sort of provisions equally
good. As to other pleasures, there is not that freedom of
conversation among the people of fashion here, that one
sees in other parts of France ; for though they are not
very numerous in this place, and consequently must live
a good deal together, yet they never come to any great
familiarity with one another. As my Lord Conway had
spent a good part of his time among them, his brother, 30

and we with him, were soon introduced into all their assemblies : As soon as you enter, the lady of the house presents each of you a card, and offers you a party at quadrille ; you sit down, and play forty deals without intermission, excepting one quarter of an hour, when every body rises to eat of what they call the *goûter*, which supplies the place of our tea, and is a service of wine, fruits, cream, sweetmeats, crawfish and cheese. People take what they like, and sit down again to play ; after
10 that, they make little parties to go to the walks together, and then all the company retire to their separate habitations. Very seldom any suppers or dinners are given ; and this is the manner they live among one another ; not so much out of any aversion they have to pleasure, as out of a sort of formality they have contracted by not being much frequented by people who have lived at Paris. It is sure they do not hate gaiety any more than the rest of their country-people, and can enter into diversions, that are once proposed, with a good grace enough ; for instance,
20 the other evening we happened to be got together in a company of eighteen people, men and women of the best fashion here, at a garden in the town to walk ; when one of the ladies bethought herself of asking, "Why should not we sup here?" Immediately the cloth was laid by the side of a fountain under the trees, and a very elegant supper served up ; after which another said, "Come, let us sing ;" and directly began herself : From singing we insensibly fell to dancing, and singing in a round ; when somebody mentioned the violins, and immediately a com-
30 pany of them was ordered : Minuets were begun in the open air, and then came country-dances, which held till four o'clock next morning ; at which hour the gayest lady there proposed, that such as were weary should get into their coaches, and the rest of them should dance before them with the music in the van ; and in this manner

we paraded through all the principal streets of the city, and waked every body in it. Mr. Walpole had a mind to make a custom of the thing, and would have given a ball in the same manner next week ; but the women did not come into it ; so I believe it will drop, and they will return to their dull cards, and usual formalities. We are not to stay above a month longer here, and shall then go to Dijon, the chief city of Burgundy, a very splendid and very gay town ; at least such is the present design.

VII.

To his Mother.

Turin, Nov. 7, N. S. 1739.

I AM this night arrived here, and have just set down to rest me after eight days tiresome journey : For the three first we had the same road we before passed through to go to Geneva ; the fourth we turned out of it, and for that day and the next travelled rather among than upon the Alps ; the way commonly running through a deep valley by the side of the river Arc, which works itself a passage, with great difficulty and a mighty noise, among vast quantities of rocks, that have rolled down from the mountain tops. The winter was so far advanced, as in great measure to spoil the beauty of the prospect ; however, there was still somewhat fine remaining amidst the savageness and horrour of the place : The sixth we began to go up several of these mountains ; and as we were passing one, met with an odd accident enough : Mr. Walpole had a little fat black spaniel, that he was very fond of, which he sometimes used to set down, and let it run by the chaise side. We were at that time in a very rough road, not two yards broad at most ; on one side was a great wood of pines, and on the other a vast precipice ; it was

noon-day, and the sun shone bright, when all of a sudden,
from the wood-side, (which was as steep upwards, as the
other part was downwards) out rushed a great wolf, came
close to the head of the horses, seized the dog by the throat,
and rushed up the hill again with him in his mouth. This
was done in less than a quarter of a minute ; we all saw
it, and yet the servants had not time to draw their pistols,
or do any thing to save the dog. If he had not been there,
and the creature had thought fit to lay hold of one of the
10 horses ; chaise, and we, and all must inevitably have
tumbled above fifty fathoms perpendicular down the
precipice. The seventh we came to Lanebourg, the last
town in Savoy ; it lies at the foot of the famous mount
Cenis, which is so situated as to allow no room for any way
but over the very top of it. Here the chaise was forced
to be pulled to pieces, and the baggage and that to be
carried by mules : We ourselves were wrapped up in our
furs, and seated upon a sort of matted chair without legs,
which is carried upon poles in the manner of a bier, and so
20 begun to ascend by the help of eight men. It was six
miles to the top, where a plain opens itself about as many
more in breadth, covered perpetually with very deep snow,
and in the midst of that a great lake of unfathomable
depth, from whence a river takes its rise, and tumbles
over monstrous rocks quite down the other side of the
mountain. The descent is six miles more, but infinitely
more steep than the going up ; and here the men perfectly
fly down with you, stepping from stone to stone with
incredible swiftness in places where none but they could
30 go three paces without falling. The immensity of the
precipices, the roaring of the river and torrents that run
into it, the huge craggs covered with ice and snow, and the
clouds below you and about you, are objects it is impossible
to conceive without seeing them ; and though we had
heard many strange descriptions of the scene, none of

them at all came up to it. We were but five hours in performing the whole, from which you may judge of the rapidity of the men's motion. We are now got into Piedmont, and stopped a little while at La Ferrière, a small village about three quarters of the way down, but still among the clouds, where we began to hear a new language spoken round about us ; at last we got quite down, went through the Pas de Suse, a narrow road among the Alps, defended by two fortresses, and lay at Bossolens : Next evening through a fine avenue of nine miles in length, as 10 straight as a line, we arrived at this city, which, as you know, is the capital of the Principality, and the residence of the King of Sardinia. * * * We shall stay here, I believe, a fortnight, and proceed for Genoa, which is three or four days journey to go post.

I am, &c.

VIII.

To Mr. West.

Turin, Nov. 16, *N. S.* 1739.

AFTER eight days journey through Greenland, we arrived at Turin. You approach it by a handsome avenue of nine miles long, and quite strait. The entrance is guarded by certain vigilant dragons, called Douâniers, who mumbled us for some time. The city is not large, as being a place 20 of strength, and consequently confined within its fortifications ; it has many beauties and some faults ; among the first are streets all laid out by the line, regular uniform buildings, fine walks that surround the whole, and in general a good lively clean appearance : But the houses are of brick plaistered, which is apt to want repairing ; the windows of oiled paper, which is apt to be torn ; and every thing very slight, which is apt to tumble down.

There is an excellent Opera, but it is only in the Carnival :
Balls every night, but only in the Carnival : Masquerades
too, but only in the Carnival. This Carnival lasts only
from Christmas to Lent ; one half of the remaining part
of the year is passed in remembering the last, the other
in expecting the future Carnival. We cannot well subsist
upon such slender diet, no more than upon an execrable
Italian Comedy, and a Puppet-Show, called *Rappresenta-
zione d'un' anima dannata*, which, I think, are all the
10 present diversions of the place ; except the Marquise de
Cavaillac's Conversazione, where one goes to see people
play at Ombre and Taroc, a game with 72 cards all painted
with suns, and moons, and devils and monks. Mr. Walpole
has been at court ; the family are at present at a country
palace, called La Vénerie. The palace here in town is the
very quintessence of gilding and looking-glass ; inlaid
floors, carved pannels, and painting, wherever they could
stick a brush. I own I have not, as yet, any where met
with those grand and simple works of Art, that are to
20 amaze one, and whose sight one is to be the better for :
But those of Nature have astonished me beyond expression. In our little journey up to the Grande Chartreuse,
I do not remember to have gone ten paces without an
exclamation, that there was no restraining : Not a precipice, not a torrent, not a cliff, but is pregnant with
religion and poetry. There are certain scenes that would
awe an atheist into belief, without the help of other argu-
ment. One need not have a very fantastic imagination to
see spirits there at noon-day ; You have Death perpetually
30 before your eyes, only so far removed, as to compose the
mind without frighting it. I am well persuaded St. Bruno
was a man of no common genius, to choose such a situation
for his retirement ; and perhaps should have been a disciple
of his, had I been born in his time. You may believe
Abelard and Heloïse were not forgot upon this occasion :

If I do not mistake, I saw you too every now and then
at a distance along the trees ; il me semble, que j'ai vu
ce chien de visage là quelque part. You seemed to call to
me from the other side of the precipice, but the noise of
the river below was so great, that I really could not distinguish what you said ; it seemed to have a cadence like
verse. In your next you will be so good to let me know
what it was. The week we have since passed among the
Alps, has not equalled the single day upon that mountain,
because the winter was rather too far advanced, and the 10
weather a little foggy. However, it did not want its
beauties ; the savage rudeness of the view is inconceivable
without seeing it : I reckoned, in one day, thirteen cascades,
the least of which was, I dare say, one hundred feet in
height. I had Livy in the chaise with me, and beheld his
" Nives cœlo propè immistæ, tecta informia imposita
" rupibus, pecora jumentaque torrida frigore, homines
" intonsi & inculti, animalia inanimaque omnia rigentia
" gelu ; omnia confragosa, præruptaque." The creatures
that inhabit them are, in all respects, below humanity ; 20
and most of them, especially women, have the tumidum
guttur, which they call goscia. Mont Cenis, I confess,
carries the permission mountains have of being frightful
rather too far ; and its horrours were accompanied with
too much danger to give one time to reflect upon their
beauties. There is a family of the Alpine monsters I have
mentioned, upon its very top, that in the middle of winter
calmly lay in their stock of provisions and firing, and so
are buried in their hut for a month or two under the snow.
When we were down it, and got a little way into Piedmont, 30
we began to find " Apricos quosdam colles, rivosque prope
" sylvas, & jam humano cultu digniora loca." I read
Silius Italicus too, for the first time ; and wished for you,
according to custom. We set out for Genoa in two days
time.

IX.

To Mr. Wharton.

Proposals for Printing by Subscription, in

THIS LARGE LETTER,

THE TRAVELS OF T. G. Gent.

WHICH WILL CONSIST OF THE FOLLOWING PARTICULARS.

Chap. I.

The Author arrives at Dover ; his conversation with the Mayor of that Corporation. Sets out in the pacquet boat : grows very sick ; the Author spews ; a very minute account of all the circumstances thereof. His arrival at Calais ; how the inhabitants of that country speak French, and are said to be all Papishes ; the Author's reflections thereupon.

II.

How they feed him with soupe, and what soupe is. How he meets with a capucin, and what a capucin is. How 10 they shut him up in a post-chaise and send him to Paris ; he goes wondering along during six days ; and how there are trees and houses just as in England. Arrives at Paris without knowing it.

III.

Full account of the river Seine, and of the various animals and plants its borders produce. Description of the little creature called an Abbé, its parts, and their uses ; with the reasons why they will not live in England, and the methods that have been used to propagate them there. A cut of the inside of a nunnery ; its structure wonderfully 20 adapted to the use of the animals that inhabit it.

IV.

Goes to the opera : grand orchestra of humstrums, bag-pipes, salt-boxes, tabours and pipes. Anatomy of a French ear, showing the formation of it to be entirely different from that of an English one ; and that sounds have a directly contrary effect upon one and the other. Fari-nelli, at Paris, said to have a fine manner, but no voice. Grand ballet, in which there is no seeing the dance for petticoats. Old women with flowers and jewels stuck in the curls of their grey hair. Red-heeled shoes and roll-ups innumerable ; hoops and panniers immeasurable, paint 10 unspeakable. Tables, wherein is calculated, with the utmost exactness, the several degrees of red, now in use, from the rising blushes of an Advocate's wife, to the flaming crimson of a Princess of the Blood ; done by a limner in great vogue.

V.

The Author takes unto him a taylour ; his character. How he covers him with silk and fringe, and widens his figure with buckram, a yard on each side. Waistcoat and breeches so strait, he can neither breathe nor walk. How the barber curls him en béquille, and à la negligée, and 20 ties a vast solitaire about his neck. How the milliner lengthens his ruffles to his fingers' ends, and sticks his two arms into a muff. How he cannot stir ; and how they cut him in proportion to his clothes.

VI.

He is carried to Versailles, despises it infinitely. A dis-sertation upon taste. Goes to an Installation in the Chapel Royal : enter the King and fifty fiddlers ; fiddlers solus ; kettle-drums and trumpets ; queens and dauphins ; prin-cesses and cardinals ; incense and the mass ; old knights making curtsies ; Holy Ghosts and fiery tongues. 30

VII.

Goes into the country to Rheims, in Champagne, stays there three months ; what he did there (he must beg the reader's pardon but) he has really forgot.

VIII.

Proceeds to Lyons, vastness of that city. Can't see the streets for houses. How rich it is, and how much it stinks. Poem upon the confluence of the Rhone and the Sâone, by a friend of the Author's ; very pretty.

IX.

Makes a journey into Savoy, and in his way visits the Grand Chartreuse : he is set aside upon a mule's back, and begins to climb up the mountains : rocks and torrents beneath, pine trees and snows above : horrours and terrours on all sides. The Author dies of the fright.

X.

He goes to Geneva. His mortal antipathy to a presbyterian, and the cure for it. Returns to Lyons ; gets a surfeit with eating ortolans and lampreys ; is advised to go into Italy for the benefit of the air.

XI.

Sets out the latter end of November to cross the Alps. He is devoured by a wolf ; and how it is to be devoured by a wolf : the seventh day he comes to the foot of Mount Cenis. How he is wrap'd up in bear-skins and beaver-skins ; boots on his legs ; caps on his head ; muffs on his hands, and taffety over his eyes. He is placed on a bier, and is carried to heaven by the savages blindfold. How he lights among a certain fat nation called Clouds ; how they are always in a sweat, and never speak, but they grunt ; how they flock about him, and think him very odd for not doing so too. He falls plump into Italy.

XII.

Arrives at Turin : goes to Genoa, and from thence to
Placentia ; crosses the river Tribia. The ghost of Hannibal
appears to him, and what it and he say upon the occasion.
Locked out of Parma on a cold winter's night ; the Author,
by an ingenious stratagem, gains admittance. Despises
that city, and proceeds through Reggio to Modena. How
the Duke and Dutchess lie over their own stables, and go
every night to a vile Italian comedy ; despises them and
it, and proceeds to Bologna.

XIII.

Enters into the dominions of the Pope o'Rome. Meets 10
the devil, and what he says on the occasion. Author longs
for Bologna sausages and hams, and how he grows as fat
as an hog.

XIV.

Observations on antiquities. The Author proves that
Bologna was the ancient Tarentum ; that the battle of
Salamis, contrary to the vulgar opinion, was fought by
land, and that not far from Ravenna ; that the Romans
were a colony of the Jews ; and that Eneas was the same
with Ehud.

XV.

Arrival at Florence. Is of opinion that the Venus of
Medicis is a modern performance, and that a very indifferent 20
one, and much inferior to the K. Charles at Charing-cross.
Account of the city and manners of the inhabitants.
A learned Dissertation on the true situation of Gomorrah.

.   .   .   .

And here will end the first part of these instructive and
entertaining voyages. The Subscribers are to pay twenty

guineas, nineteen down, and the remainder upon delivery of the book. N. B. A few are printed on the softest royal brown paper, for the use of the curious.

MY DEAR, DEAR WHARTON,

(WHICH is a dear more than I give any body else. It is very odd to begin with a parenthesis, but) You may think me a beast not having sooner wrote to you, and to be sure a beast I am. Now, when one owns it, I don't see what you have left to say. I take this opportunity
10 to inform you (an opportunity I have had every week this twelvemonth) that I am arrived safe at Calais, and am at present at—Florence, a city in Italy, in I don't know how many degrees of N. latitude. Under the line I am sure it is not, for I am at this instant expiring with cold. You must know, that not being certain what circumstances of my history would particularly suit your curiosity, and knowing that all I had to say to you would overflow the narrow limits of many a good quire of paper, I have taken this method of laying before you the contents, that you
20 may pitch upon what you please, and give me your orders accordingly to expatiate thereupon : for I conclude you will write to me : won't you ? oh ! yes, when you know that in a week I set out for Rome, and that the Pope is dead, and that I shall be (I should say, God willing ; and if nothing extraordinary intervene ; and if I am alive and well ; and in all human probability) at the coronation of a new one. Now, as you have no other correspondent there, and as if you do not, I certainly shall not write again. (Observe my impudence.) I take it to be your
30 interest to send me a vast letter, full of all sorts of news and politics, and such other ingredients, as to you shall seem convenient with all decent expedition, only do not be too severe upon the Pretender ; and if you like my

style, pray say so. This is à la Françoise ; and if your
think it a little too foolish, and impertinent, you shall be
treated alla Toscana with a thousand Signoria Illustrissi-
mas, in the mean time I have the honour to remain

Your lofing frind, tell deth,

T. GRAY.

Florence, March 12, *N. S.* 1740.

P. S. This is à l'Angloise. I don't know where you are ;
if at Cambridge pray let me know all, how, and about it :
and if my old friends, Thomson or Clarke, fall in your
way, say I am extremely theirs. But if you are in town, 10
I entreat you to make my best compliments to Mrs. Wharton. Adieu.

Yours, sincerely, a second time.

X.

To his Mother.

Naples, June 17, 1740.

OUR journey hither was through the most beautiful part
of the finest country in the world ; and every spot of it,
on some account or other, famous for these three thousand
years past. The season has hitherto been just as warm
as one would wish it ; no unwholesome airs, or violent
heats, yet heard of : The people call it a backward year,
and are in pain about their corn, wine, and oil ; but we, 20
who are neither corn, wine, nor oil, find it very agreeable.
Our road was through Velletri, Cisterna, Terracina, Capua,
and Aversa, and so to Naples. The minute one leaves his
Holiness's dominions, the face of things begins to change
from wide uncultivated plains to olive groves and well-
tilled fields of corn, intermixed with ranks of elms, every
one of which has its vine twining about it, and hanging

in festoons between the rows from one tree to another.
The great old fig-trees, the oranges in full bloom, and
myrtles in every hedge, make one of the delightfullest
scenes you can conceive ; besides that, the roads are wide,
well-kept, and full of passengers, a sight I have not beheld
this long time. My wonder still increased upon entering
the city, which I think, for number of people, outdoes
both Paris and London. The streets are one continued
market, and thronged with populace so much that a coach
10 can hardly pass. The common sort are a jolly lively kind
of animals, more industrious than Italians usually are ;
they work till evening ; then take their lute or guitar (for
they all play) and walk about the city, or upon the sea-
shore with it, to enjoy the fresco. One sees their little
brown children jumping about stark-naked, and the bigger
ones dancing with castanets, while others play on the
cymbal to them. Your maps will show you the situation
of Naples ; it is on the most lovely bay in the world, and
one of the calmest seas : It has many other beauties
20 besides those of nature. We have spent two days in
visiting the remarkable places in the country round it,
such as the bay of Baiæ, and its remains of antiquity ; the
lake Avernus, and the Solfatara, Charon's grotto, &c.
We have been in the Sybil's cave and many other strange
holes underground (I only name them, because you may
consult Sandy's *Travels*) ; but the strangest hole I ever
was in, has been to-day at a place called Portici, where
his Sicilian Majesty has a country-seat. About a year ago,
as they were digging, they discovered some parts of ancient
30 buildings above thirty feet deep in the ground : Curiosity
led them on, and they have been digging ever since ; the
passage they have made, with all its turnings and windings,
is now more than a mile long. As you walk, you see parts
of an amphitheatre, many houses adorned with marble
columns, and incrusted with the same ; the front of

a temple, several arched vaults of rooms painted in fresco. Some pieces of painting have been taken out from hence, finer than any thing of the kind before discovered, and with these the king has adorned his palace ; also a number of statues, medals, and gems ; and more are dug out every day. This is known to be a Roman town, that in the emperor Titus's time was overwhelmed by a furious eruption of Mount Vesuvius, which is hard by. The wood and beams remain so perfect that you may see the grain ; but burnt to a coal, and dropping into dust upon the least 10 touch. We were to-day at the foot of that mountain, which at present smokes only a little, where we saw the materials that fed the stream of fire, which about four years since ran down its side. We have but a few days longer to stay here ; too little in conscience for such a place. * * *

XI.

To Mr. West.

Florence, July 16, 1740.

You do yourself and me justice, in imagining that you merit, and that I am capable of sincerity. I have not a thought, or even a weakness, I desire to conceal from you ; and consequently on my side deserve to be treated 20 with the same openness of heart. My vanity perhaps might make me more reserved towards you, if you were one of the heroic race, superior to all human failings ; but as mutual wants are the ties of general society, so are mutual weaknesses of private friendships, supposing them mixt with some proportion of good qualities ; for where one may not sometimes blame, one does not much care ever to praise. All this has the air of an introduction designed to soften a very harsh reproof that is to follow ;

but it is no such matter : I only meant to ask, Why did
you change your lodging ? Was the air bad, or the situation melancholy ? If so, you are quite in the right. Only,
is it not putting yourself a little out of the way of a people,
with whom it seems necessary to keep up some sort of
intercourse and conversation, though but little for your
pleasure or entertainment, (yet there are, I believe, such
among them as might give you both) at least for your
information in that study, which, when I left you, you
10 thought of applying to ? for that there is a certain study
necessary to be followed, if we mean to be of any use in
the world, I take for granted ; disagreeable enough (as
most necessities are) but, I am afraid, unavoidable. Into
how many branches these studies are divided in England,
every body knows ; and between that which you and I had
pitched upon, and the other two, it was impossible to
balance long. Examples shew one that it is not absolutely
necessary to be a blockhead to succeed in this profession.
The labour is long, and the elements dry and unentertaining ;
20 nor was ever any body (especially those that afterwards
made a figure in it) amused, or even not disgusted in the
beginning ; yet, upon a further acquaintance, there is
surely matter for curiosity and reflection. It is strange if,
among all that huge mass of words, there be not somewhat
intermixed for thought. Laws have been the result of
long deliberation, and that not of dull men, but the contrary ; and have so close a connection with history, nay,
with philosophy itself, that they must partake a little of
what they are related to so nearly. Besides, tell me, have
30 you ever made the attempt ? Was not you frighted merely
with the distant prospect ? Had the Gothic character
and bulkiness of those volumes (a tenth part of which
perhaps it will be no further necessary to consult, than as
one does a dictionary) no ill effect upon your eye ? Are
you sure, if Coke had been printed by Elzevir, and bound

in twenty neat pocket volumes, instead of one folio, you should never have taken him for an hour, as you would a Tully, or drank your tea over him ? I know how great an obstacle ill spirits are to resolution. Do you really think, if you rid ten miles every morning, in a week's time you should not entertain much stronger hopes of the Chancellorship, and think it a much more probable thing than you do at present ? The advantages you mention are not nothing ; our inclinations are more than we imagine in our own power ; reason and resolution determine them, 10 and support under many difficulties. To me there hardly appears to be any medium between a public life and a private one ; he who prefers the first, must put himself in a way of being serviceable to the rest of mankind, if he has a mind to be of any consequence among them : Nay, he must not refuse being in a certain degree even dependent upon some men who are so already. If he has the good fortune to light on such as will make no ill use of his humility, there is no shame in this : If not, his ambition ought to give place to a reasonable pride, and he should 20 apply to the cultivation of his own mind those abilities which he has not been permitted to use for others' service. Such a private happiness (supposing a small competence of fortune) is almost always in every one's power, and the proper enjoyment of age, as the other is the employment of youth. You are yet young, have some advantages and opportunities, and an undoubted capacity, which you have never yet put to the trial. Set apart a few hours, see how the first year will agree with you, at the end of it you are still the master ; if you change your mind, you will only 30 have got the knowledge of a little somewhat that can do no hurt, or give you cause of repentance. If your inclination be not fixed upon any thing else, it is a symptom that you are not absolutely determined against this, and warns you not to mistake mere indolence for inability. I am

sensible there is nothing stronger against what I would
persuade you to, than my own practice ; which may make
you imagine I think not as I speak. Alas ! it is not so ;
but I do not act what I think, and I had rather be the
object of your pity, than you should be that of mine ;
and, be assured, the advantage that I may receive from
it, does not diminish my concern in hearing you want
somebody to converse with freely, whose advice might be
of more weight, and always at hand. We have some time
10 since come to the southern period of our voyages ; we
spent about nine days at Naples. It is the largest and
most populous city, as its environs are the most deliciously
fertile country, of all Italy. We sailed in the bay of Baiæ,
sweated in the Solfatara, and died in the grotto del Cane,
as all strangers do ; saw the Corpus Christi procession,
and the King and the Queen, and the city underground,
(which is a wonder I reserve to tell you of another time)
and so returned to Rome for another fortnight ; left it
(left Rome !) and came hither for the summer. You have
20 seen an Epistle to Mr. Ashton that seems to me full of
spirit and thought, and a good deal of poetic fire. I would
know your opinion. Now I talk of verses, Mr. Walpole
and I have frequently wondered you should never mention
a certain imitation of Spenser, published last year by
a namesake of yours, with which we are all enraptured
and enmarvailed.

XII.

To Mr. West.

Florence, April 21, 1741.

I KNOW not what degree of satisfaction it will give you
to be told that we shall set out from hence the 24th of
this month, and not stop above a fortnight at any place
in our way. This I feel, that you are the principal
pleasure I have to hope for in my own country. Try at
least to make me imagine myself not indifferent to you ; for
I must own I have the vanity of desiring to be esteemed
by somebody, and would choose that somebody should be
one whom I esteem as much as I do you. As I am recom-
mending myself to your love, methinks I ought to send 10
you my picture (for I am no more what I was, some circumstances excepted, which I hope I need not particularize
to you) ; you must add then, to your former idea, two
years of age, a reasonable quantity of dullness, a great
deal of silence, and something that rather resembles, than
is, thinking ; a confused notion of many strange and fine
things that have swum before my eyes for some time,
a want of love for general society, indeed an inability to
it. On the good side you may add a sensibility for what
others feel, and indulgence for their faults and weaknesses, 20
a love of truth, and detestation of every thing else. Then
you are to deduct a little impertinence, a little laughter,
a great deal of pride, and some spirits. These are all the
alterations I know of, you perhaps may find more. Think
not that I have been obliged for this reformation of manners
to reason or reflection, but to a severer school-mistress,
Experience. One has little merit in learning her lessons,
for one cannot well help it ; but they are more useful
than others, and imprint themselves in the very heart.

I find I have been haranguing in the style of the Son of
Sirach, so shall finish here, and tell you that our route is
settled as follows : First to Bologna for a few days, to hear
the Viscontina sing ; next to Reggio, where is a Fair.
Now, you must know, a Fair here is not a place where
one eats gingerbread or rides upon hobby-horses ; here
are no musical clocks, nor tall Leicestershire women ; one
has nothing but masquing, gaming, and singing. If you
love operas, there will be the most splendid in Italy, four
10 tip-top voices, a new theatre, the Duke and Dutchess in
all their pomps and vanities. Does not this sound magnificent ? Yet is the city of Reggio but one step above Old
Brentford. Well ; next to Venice by the 11th of May,
there to see the old Doge wed the Adriatic Whore. Then
to Verona, so to Milan, so to Marseilles, so to Lyons, so to
Paris, so to West, &c. in sæcula sæculorum. Amen.

Eleven months, at different times, have I passed at
Florence ; and yet (God help me) know not either people
or language. Yet the place and the charming prospects
20 demand a poetical farewell, and here it is.

*   *   *   *   *   *

XIII.

To Mr. West.

London, April, Thursday [1742].

You are the first who ever made a Muse of a Cough ;
to me it seems a much more easy task to versify in one's
sleep, (that indeed you were of old famous for) than for
want of it. Not the wakeful nightingale (when she had
a cough) ever sung so sweetly. I give you thanks for your
warble, and wish you could sing yourself to rest. These
wicked remains of your illness will sure give way to warm
weather and gentle exercise ; which I hope you will not

omit as the season advances. Whatever low spirits and
indolence, the effect of them, may advise to the contrary,
I pray you add five steps to your walk daily for my sake ;
by the help of which, in a month's time, I propose to set
you on horseback.

I talked of the *Dunciad* as concluding you had seen it ;
if you have not, do you choose I should get and send it
you ? I have myself, upon your recommendation, been
reading *Joseph Andrews*. The incidents are ill laid and
without invention ; but the characters have a great deal 10
of nature, which always pleases even in her lowest shapes.
Parson Adams is perfectly well ; so is Mrs. Slipslop, and
the story of Wilson ; and throughout he shews himself
well read in Stage-Coaches, Country Squires, Inns, and Inns
of Court. His reflections upon high people and low people,
and misses and masters, are very good. However the
exaltedness of some minds (or rather as I shrewdly suspect
their insipidity and want of feeling or observation) may
make them insensible to these light things, (I mean such
as characterize and paint nature) yet surely they are as 20
weighty and much more useful than your grave discourses
upon the mind, the passions, and what not. Now as the
paradisaical pleasures of the Mahometans consist in playing upon the flute and lying with Houris, be mine to read
eternal new romances of Marivaux and Crebillon.

You are very good in giving yourself the trouble to read
and find fault with my long harangues. Your freedom (as
you call it) has so little need of apologies, that I should
scarce excuse your treating me any otherwise ; which,
whatever compliment it might be to my vanity, would be 30
making a very ill one to my understanding. As to matter
of stile, I have this to say : The language of the age is
never the language of poetry ; except among the French,
whose verse, where the thought or image does not support
it, differs in nothing from prose. Our poetry on the

contrary, has a language peculiar to itself ; to which almost
every one, that has written, has added something by
enriching it with foreign idioms and derivatives: Nay
sometimes words of their own composition or invention.
Shakespear and Milton have been great creators this way ;
and no one more licentious than Pope or Dryden, who
perpetually borrow expressions from the former. Let me
give you some instances from Dryden, whom every body
reckons a great master of our poetical tongue.——Full of
10 *museful mopeings*—unlike the *trim* of love—a pleasant
beverage—a *roundelay* of love—stood silent in his *mood*—
with knots and *knares* deformed—his *ireful mood*—in
proud *array*—his *boon* was granted—and *disarray* and
shameful rout—*wayward* but wise—*furbished* for the field
—the *foiled dodderd* oaks—*disherited*—*smouldring* flames—
retchless of laws—*crones* old and ugly—the *beldam* at his
side—the *grandam-hag*—*villanize* his father's fame.——
But they are infinite : And our language not being a settled
thing (like the French) has an undoubted right to words
20 of an hundred years old, provided antiquity have not
rendered them unintelligible.   In truth, Shakespear's
language is one of his principal beauties ; and he has no
less advantage over your Addisons and Rowes in this,
than in those other great excellences you mention. Every
word in him is a picture.   Pray put me the following lines
into the tongue of our modern Dramatics :

> But I, that am not shaped for sportive tricks,
> Nor made to court an amorous looking-glass :
> I, that am rudely stampt, and want love's majesty
30 To strut before a wanton ambling nymph :
> I, that am curtail'd of this fair proportion,
> Cheated of feature by dissembling nature,
> Deform'd, unfinish'd, sent before my time
> Into this breathing world, scarce half made up—

and what follows.   To me they appear untranslatable ;
and if this be the case, our language is greatly degenerated.

However, the affectation of imitating Shakespear may doubtless be carried too far ; and is no sort of excuse for sentiments ill-suited, or speeches ill-timed, which I believe is a little the case with me. I guess the most faulty expressions may be these—*silken* son of *dalliance*—*drowsier* pretensions—wrinkled *beldams*—*arched* the hearer's brow and *riveted* his eyes in *fearful extasie*. These are easily altered or omitted : and indeed if the thoughts be wrong or superfluous, there is nothing easier than to leave out the whole. The first ten or twelve lines are, I believe, the best ; 10 and as for the rest, I was betrayed into a good deal of it by Tacitus ; only what he has said in five words, I imagine I have said in fifty lines. Such is the misfortune of imitating the inimitable. Now, if you are of my opinion, una litura may do the business better than a dozen ; and you need not fear unravelling my web. I am a sort of spider ; and have little else to do but spin it over again, or creep to some other place and spin there. Alas ! for one who has nothing to do but amuse himself, I believe my amusements are as little amusing as most folks. But no matter ; it makes 20 the hours pass ; and is better than ἐν ἀμαθίᾳ καὶ ἀμουσίᾳ καταβιῶναι.

Adieu.

XIV.

To Mr. West.

(*Extract.*)

London, May 27, 1742.

MINE, you are to know, is a white Melancholy, or rather Leucocholy for the most part ; which though it seldom laughs or dances, nor ever amounts to what one calls Joy or Pleasure, yet is a good easy sort of a state, and ça ne laisse que de s'amuser. The only fault of it's insipidity ;

which is apt now and then to give a sort of Ennui, which makes one form certain little wishes that signify nothing. But there is another sort, black indeed, which I have now and then felt, that has somewhat in it like Tertullian's rule of faith, Credo quia impossibile est; for it believes, nay, is sure of every thing that is unlikely, so it be but frightful; and on the other hand, excludes and shuts its eyes to the most possible hopes, and every thing that is pleasurable; from this the Lord deliver us! for none but he and sunshiny weather can do it. In hopes of enjoying this kind of weather, I am going into the country for a few weeks, but shall be never the nearer any society; so, if you have any charity, you will continue to write. My life is like Harry the Fourth's supper of Hens, " Poulets à la " broche, Poulets en Ragôut, Poulets en Hâchis, Poulets " en Fricasées." Reading here, Reading there; nothing but books with different sauces. Do not let me lose my desert then; for though that be Reading too, yet it has a very different flavour. The May seems to be come since your invitation; and I propose to bask in her beams and dress me in her roses.

Et Caput in vernâ semper habere rosâ.

I shall see Mr. * * and his Wife, nay, and his Child too, for he has got a Boy. Is it not odd to consider one's Cotemporaries in the grave light of Husband and Father? There is my Lords Sandwich and Halifax, they are Statesmen: Do not you remember them dirty boys playing at cricket? As for me, I am never a bit the older, nor the bigger, nor the wiser than I was then: No, not for having been beyond sea. Pray how are you?

XV.

To Mr. Wharton.

Stoke, Thursday, 16th Nov. [1745].

I AM not lost ; here am I at Stoke, whither I came on
Tuesday, and shall be again in town on Saturday, and at
Cambridge on Wednesday or Thursday, you may be
anxious to know what has past. I wrote a note the night
I came, and immediately received a very civil answer.
I went the following evening to see the *party,* (as Mrs. Foible
says) was something abashed at his confidence : he came
to meet me, kissed me on both sides with all the ease of
one, who receives an acquaintance just come out of the
country, squatted me into a Fauteuïl, begun to talk of the 10
town, and this and that and t'other, and continued with
little interruption for three hours, when I took my leave
very indifferently pleased, but treated with monstrous good-
breeding. I supped with him next night, (as he desired) ;
Ashton was there, whose formalities tickled me inwardly,
for he, (I found) was to be angry about the letter I had
wrote him. However in going home together our hackney-
coach jumbled us into a sort of reconciliation : he hammered
out somewhat like an excuse, and I received it very readily,
because I cared not twopence, whether it were true or not. 20
So we grew the best acquaintance imaginable, and I sate
with him on Sunday some hours alone, when he informed
me of abundance of anecdotes much to my satisfaction,
and in short opened (I really believe) his heart to me, with
that sincerity that I found I had still less reason to have
a good opinion of him than (if possible) I ever had before.
Next morning I breakfasted alone with Mr. Walpole ;
when we had all the éclaircissement I ever expected, and
I left him far better satisfied than I have been hitherto.
When I return I shall see him again. 30

Such is the epitome of my four days. Mr. and Mrs. Simms and Mad^lle· Nanny have done the honours of Leaden Hall to a miracle, and all join in a compliment to the Doctor. Your brother is well, the books are in good condition. Mad^me· Chenevix has frighted me with Ecritoires she asks three guineas for, that are not worth three half-pence : I have been in several shops and found nothing pretty. I fear it must be bespoke at last.

The day after I went you received a little letter directed
10 to me, that seems wrote with a skewer, please to open it, and you will find a receipt of Dan. Adcock for ten pound, which I will beg you to receive of Gillham for me. If the letter miscarried, pray take care the money is paid to no one else. I expect to have a letter from you when I come to town, at your lodgings.

Adieu, Sir, I am sincerely yours,

T. G.

XVI.

To Mr. Walpole.

Cambridge, February 3, 1746.

DEAR SIR,

You are so good to enquire after my usual time of
20 coming to town : it is a season when even you, the perpetual friend of London, will, I fear, hardly be in it—the middle of June : and I commonly return hither in September ; a month when I may more probably find you at home.

Our defeat to be sure is a rueful affair for the honour of the troops ; but the Duke is gone it seems with the rapidity of a cannon-bullet to undefeat us again. The common people in town at least know how to be afraid : but we are such uncommon people here as to have no more sense óf danger than if the battle had been **fought** when and where the battle of Cannæ was.

The perception of these calamities, and of their consequences, that we are supposed to get from books, is so faintly impressed, that we talk of war, famine, and pestilence, with no more apprehension than of a broken head, or of a coach overturned between York and Edinburgh.

I heard three people, sensible middle aged men (when the Scotch were said to be at Stamford, and actually were at Derby,) talking of hiring a chaise to go to Caxton 10 (a place in the high road) to see the Pretender and the Highlanders as they passed.

I can say no more for Mr. Pope (for what you keep in reserve may be worse than all the rest.) It is natural to wish the finest writer, one of them, we ever had, should be an honest man. It is for the interest even of that virtue, whose friend he professed himself, and whose beauties he sung, that he should not be found a dirty animal. But however, this is Mr. Warburton's business, not mine, who may scribble his pen to the stumps and all 20 in vain, if these facts are so. It is not from what he told me about himself that I thought well of him, but from a humanity, and goodness of heart, aye, and greatness of mind, that runs through his private correspondence, not less apparent than are a thousand little vanities and weaknesses mixed with those good qualities, for nobody ever took him for a philosopher. If you know any thing of Mr. Mann's state of health and happiness, or the motions of Mr. Chute homewards, it will be a particular favour to inform me of them, as I have not heard this half-year 30 from them.

I am sincerely yours,

T. GRAY.

XVII.

To Mr. Wharton.

Cambridge, Thursday, April 26, 1745.

YOU write so feelingly to little Mr. Brown, and represent your abandoned condition in terms so touching, that what gratitude could not effect in several months, compassion has brought about in a few days, and broke that strong attachment, or rather allegiance which I and all here owe to our sovereign lady and mistress, the president of presidents, and head of heads (if I may be permitted to pronounce her name, that ineffable Octogrammaton) the power of *Laziness*. You must know she had been pleased to
10 appoint me (in preference to so many old servants of hers, who had spent their whole lives in qualifying themselves for the office) grand picker of straws, and push-pin player in ordinary to her Supinity, (for that is her title) the first is much in the nature of lord president of the council, and the other, like the groom-porter, only without the profit ; but as they are both things of very great honour in this country, I considered with myself the load of envy attending such great charges, and besides (between you and I) I found myself unable to support the fatigue of keeping
20 up the appearance, that persons of such dignity must do, so I thought proper to decline it, and excused myself as well as I could ; however as you see such an affair must take up a good deal of time, and it has always been the policy of this court to proceed slowly, like the Imperial, and that of Spain, in the dispatch of business ; so that you will the easier forgive me, if I have not answered your letter before.

You desire to know, it seems, what character the Poem of your young friend bears here. I wonder to hear you
30 ask the opinion of a nation, where those who pretend to judge, don't judge at all ; and the rest (the wiser part)

wait to catch the judgment of the world immediately above them, that is, Dick's coffee-house, and the Rainbow ; so that the readier way would be to ask Mrs. This and Mrs. T'other, that keeps the bar there. However to shew you I'm a judge, as well as my countrymen, though I have rather turned it over than read it, (but no matter : no more have they) it seems to me above the middleing, and now and then (but for a little while) rises even to the best, particularly in description. It is often obscure, and even unintelligible, and too much infected with the Hutcheson 10 jargon ; in short it's great fault is that it was published at least nine years too early ; and so methinks in a few words, à la mode du temple, I have very nearly dispatched what may perhaps for several years have employed a very ingenious man, worth fifty of myself. Here is a poem called the *Enthusiast*, which is all pure description, and as they tell me by the same hand. Is it so or not ? Item a more bulky one upon Health, wrote by a physician : do you know him ? *Master Tommy Lucretius* (since you are so good to enquire after the child) is but a puleing chitt 20 yet, not a bit grown to speak of ; I believe, poor thing ! it has got the worms, that will carry it off at last. Oh Lord ! I forgot to tell you, that Mr. Trollope and I are under a course of tar water, he for his present, and I for my future distempers ; if you think it will kill me, send away a man and horse directly, for I drink like a fish. I should be glad to know how your ———— goes on, and give you joy of it.

You are much in the right to have a taste for Socrates, he was a divine man. I must tell you, by way of the news of the place, that the other day, Mr. Traigneau (entering 30 upon his Professorship) made an apology for him an hour long in the schools, and all the world, except Trinity College, brought in Socrates guilty.

Adieu, dear Sir, and believe me
Your Friend and Servant,

T. G.

XVIII.

To Mr. Wharton.

(Extract.)

Stoke, Sunday, 13th August, 1746.

MY DEAR WHARTON,

MY evenings have been chiefly spent at Ranelagh and
Vauxhall, several of my mornings, or rather noons, in
Arlington-street, and the rest at the tryal of the Lords.
The first day I was not there, and only saw the Lord High
Steward's parade in going ; the second and third * * * * * * *
Peers were all in their robes * * * * * by their wearing bag-
wigs and hats instead of coronets. The Lord High-Steward
was the least part of the shew, as he wore only his baron's
10 robe, and was always asking the heralds what he should
do next, and bowing or smileing about to his acquaintance :
as to his speech, you see it ; people hold it very cheap,
though several incorrectnesses have been altered in the
printed copy. Kilmarnock spoke in mitigation of his crime
near half an hour, with a decent courage, and in a strong,
but pathetic voice. His figure would prejudice people in
his favour, being tall and genteel ; he is upwards of forty,
but to the eye not above thirty-five years of age. What
he said appears to less advantage when read. Cromartie,
20 (who is about the same age, a man of lower stature, but
much like a gentleman), was sinking into the earth with
grief and dejection ; with eyes cast down, and a voice so
low, that no one heard a syllable that did not sit close to
the bar ; he made a short speech to raise compassion. It
is now I see printed, and is reckoned extremely fine.
I believe you will think it touching and well expressed :
if there be any meanness in it, it is lost in that sorrow he
gives us for so numerous and helpless a family. Lady

Cromartie (who is said to have drawn her husband into these circumstances) was at Leicester House on Wednesday, with four of her children. The Princess saw her, and made no other answer than by bringing in her own children and placing them by her ; which (if true) is one of the prettiest things I ever heard. She was also at the Duke's, who refused to admit her ; but she waited till he came to his coach, and threw herself at his knees, while her children hung upon him, till he promised her all his interest could do ; and before, on several occasions, he has been heard to speak very mildly of Cromartie, and very severely of Kilmarnock ; so if any be spared, it will probably be the former, though he had a pension of £600 a year from the government, and the order for giving quarter to no Englishman was found in his pocket. As to Balmerino, he never had any hopes from the beginning. He is an old soldier-like man, of a vulgar manner and aspect, speaks the broadest Scotch, and shows an intrepidity, that some ascribe to real courage, and some to brandy. You have heard perhaps, that the first day, (while the Peers were adjourned to consider of his plea, and he left alone for an hour and a half in the bar) he diverted himself with the ax, that stood by him, played with it's tassels, and tryed the edge with his finger : and some lord, as he passed by him, saying he was surprized to hear him alledge any thing so frivolous, and that could not possibly do him the least service ; he answered, that as there were so many ladies present, he thought it would be uncivil to give them no amusement. The Duke of Argyle, telling him, how sorry and how astonished he was to see him engaged in such a cause ; My Lord (says he) for the two Kings, and their rights, I cared not a farthing which prevailed ; but I was starving ; and by God, if Mahomet had set up his standard in the Highlands, I had been a good Mussulman for bread, and stuck close to the party, for I must eat.

The Solicitor-General came up to speak to him too, and he turns about to old Williamson. Who is that Lawyer that talks to me ? My Lord, it is Mr. Murray. Ha ! Mr. Murray, my good Friend, (says he, and shook him by the hand) and how does your good mother ? oh ! she was of admirable service to us ; we should have done nothing without her in Perthshire. He recommends (he says) his Peggy ('tis uncertain * * * * the favour of the Government, for she has * * *.

10 I have been diverted with an account of Lord Lovat in his confinement at Edinburgh. There was a Captain Maggett, that is obliged to lie in the room every night with him. When first he was introduced to him, he made him come to his bed-side, where he lay in a hundred flannel waistcoats, and a furred night-gown, took him in his arms, and gave him a long embrace, that absolutely suffocated him. He will speak nothing but French ; insists upon it that Maggett is a Frenchman, and calls him mon cher Capitaine Magot (you know *Magot* is a monkey). At his 20 head lie two Highland women, at his feet two Highland men. By his bed-side is a close-stool, to which he rises two or three times in a night, and always says,—Ah, mon cher Capitaine Magot ! vous m'excuserez, mais la Nature demande que je chie ! He is to be impeached by the House of Commons, because not being actually in arms, it would otherwise be necessary that the jury of Inverness should find a Bill of Indictment against him, which it is very sure they would not do. When the Duke returned to Edinburgh they refused to admit Kingston's Light 30 Horse, and talked of their privileges, but they came in sword in hand, and replied, that when the Pretender was at their gates, they had said nothing of their privileges. The Duke rested some hours there, but refused to see the magistracy. I believe you may think it full time, that I close my budget of stories : Mr. Walpole I have seen

a good deal, and shall do a good deal more, I suppose, for
he is looking for a house somewhere about Windsor during
the Summer.   All is mighty free, and even friendly more
than one could expect.

XIX.

To Mr. Walpole.

Cambridge, 1747.

I HAD been absent from this place a few days, and at
my return found Cibber's book upon my table : I return
you my thanks for it, and have already run over a considerable part ; for who could resist Mrs. Letitia Pilkington's recommendation ? (by the way is there any such
gentlewoman ? or has somebody put on the style of a 10
scribbling woman's panegyric to deceive and laugh at
Colley ?)   He seems to me full as pert and as dull as usual.
There are whole pages of common-place stuff, that for
stupidity might have been wrote by Dr. Waterland, or
any other grave divine, did not the flirting saucy phrase
give them at a distance an air of youth and gaiety : It is
very true, he is often in the right with regard to Tully's
weaknesses ; but was there any one that did not see them ?
Those, I imagine, that would find a man after God's own
heart, are no more likely to trust the Doctor's recom- 20
mendation than the Player's ;   and as to Reason and
Truth would they know their own faces, do you think,
if they looked in the glass, and saw themselves so bedizened
in tattered fringe and tarnished lace, in French jewels,
and dirty furbelows, the frippery of a stroller's wardrobe ?
    Literature, to take it in its most comprehensive sense,
and include every thing that requires invention or judgement, or barely application and industry, seems indeed
drawing apace to its dissolution, and remarkably since the
beginning of the war.   I remember to have read Mr. Spence's 30

pretty book ; though (as he then had not been at Rome
for the last time) it must have increased greatly since that
in bulk. If you ask me what I read, I protest I do not
recollect one syllable ; but only in general, that they were
the best bred sort of men in the world, just the kind of
frinds one would wish to meet in a fine summer's evening,
if one wished to meet any at all. The heads and tails of
the dialogues, published separate in 16mo, would make the
sweetest reading in *natiur* for young gentlemen of family
10 and fortune, that are learning to dance. I rejoice to hear
there is such a crowd of dramatical performances coming
upon the stage. *Agrippina* can stay very well, she thanks
you, and be damned at leisure : I hope in God you have
not mentioned, or shewed to any body that scene (for
trusting in its badness, I forgot to caution you concerning
it) ; but I heard the other day, that I was writing a Play,
and was told the name of it, which nobody here could
know, I am sure. The employment you propose to me
much better suits my inclination ; but I much fear our
20 joint-stock would hardly compose a small volume ; what
I have is less considerable than you would imagine, and of
that little we should not be unwilling to publish all. * * *

This is all I can any where find. You, I imagine, may
have a good deal more. I should not care how unwise the
ordinary run of Readers might think my affection for him,
provided those few, that ever loved any body, or judged of
any thing rightly, might, from such little remains, be moved
to consider what he would have been ; and to wish that
heaven had granted him a longer life and a mind more at ease.

30 I send you a few lines, though Latin, which you do not
like, for the sake of the subject ; it makes part of a large
design, and is the beginning of the fourth book, which
was intended to treat of the passions. Excuse the three
first verses ; you know vanity, with the Romans, is a
poetical licence.

XX.

To Mr. Walpole.

Cambridge, March 1, 1747.

As one ought to be particularly careful to avoid blunders in a compliment of condolence, it would be a sensible satisfaction to me (before I testify my sorrow, and the sincere part I take in your misfortune) to know for certain, who it is I lament. I knew Zara and Selima, (Selima, was it ? or Fatima ?) or rather I knew them both together ; for I cannot justly say which was which. Then as to your handsome Cat, the name you distinguish her by, I am no less at a loss, as well knowing one's handsome cat is always the cat one likes best ; or if one be alive and the other dead, it is usually the latter that is the handsomest. Besides, if the point were never so clear, I hope you do not think me so ill-bred or so imprudent as to forfeit all my interest in the survivor : Oh no ! I would rather seem to mistake, and imagine to be sure it must be the tabby one that had met with this sad accident. Till this affair is a little better determined, you will excuse me if I do not begin to cry ;

" Tempus inane peto, requiem, spatiumque doloris."

Which interval is the more convenient, as it gives time to rejoice with you on your new honors. This is only a beginning ; I reckon next week we shall hear you are a Free-Mason, or a Gormogon at least.—Heigh ho ! I feel (as you to be sure have done long since) that I have very little to say, at least in prose. Somebody will be the better for it ; I do not mean you, but your Cat, feuë Mademoiselle Selime, whom I am about to immortalize for one week or fortnight, as follows

*   *   *   *   *   *   *

There's a Poem for you, it is rather too long for an Epitaph.

XXI.

To Mr. Walpole.

January or February 1748.

I AM obliged to you for Mr. Dodsley's book, and having pretty well looked it over, will (as you desire) tell you my opinion of it. He might, methinks, have spared the graces in his frontispiece, if he chose to be economical, and dressed his authors in a little more decent raiment—not in whited-brown paper, and distorted characters, like an old ballad. I am ashamed to see myself ; but the company keeps me in countenance : so to begin with Mr. Tickell. This is not only a state-poem (my ancient aversion), but
10 a state-poem on the peace of Utrecht. If Mr. Pope had wrote a panegyric on it, one could hardly have read him with patience : but this is only a poor short-winded imitator of Addison, who had himself not above three or four notes in poetry, sweet enough indeed, like those of a German flute, but such as soon tire and satiate the ear with their frequent return. Tickell has added to this a great poverty of sense, and a string of transitions that hardly become a school-boy. However I forgive him for the sake of his ballad, which I always thought the prettiest
20 in the world.

All there is of M. Green here, has been printed before ; there is a profusion of wit every where ; reading would have formed his judgement, and harmonized his verse, for even his wood-notes often break out into strains of real poetry and music. *The School Mistress* is excellent in its kind and masterly ; and (I am sorry to differ from you,

but) *London* is to me one of those few imitations that have
all the ease and all the spirit of an original. The same
man's verses on the opening of Garrick's theatre are far
from bad. Mr. Dyer (here you will despise me highly)
has more of poetry in his imagination than almost any of
our number ; but rough and injudicious. I should range
Mr. Bramston only a step or two above Dr. King, who is
as low in my estimation as in yours. Dr. Evans is a furious
madman ; and pre-existence is nonsense in all her altitudes.
Mr. Lyttelton is a gentle elegiac person. Mr. Nugent sure
did not write his own Ode. I like Mr. Whitehead's little
poems, I mean the *Ode on a Tent*, the *Verses to Garrick*,
and particularly those *to Charles Townsend*, better than
any thing I had seen before of him. I gladly pass over
H. Browne and the rest, to come at you. You know I was
of the publishing side, and thought your reasons against
it none ; for though, as Mr. Chute said extremely well,
the *still small voice* of Poetry was not made to be heard
in a crowd ; yet satire will be heard, for all the audience
are by nature her friends ; especially when she appears in
the spirit of Dryden, with his strength, and often with his
versification, such as you have caught in those lines on
the Royal Unction, on the Papal Dominion, and Convents
of both Sexes, on Henry VIII. and Charles II. ; for these
are to me the shining parts of your *Epistle*. There are
many lines I could wish corrected, and some blotted out,
but beauties enough to atone for a thousand worse faults
than these. The opinion of such as can at all judge, who
saw it before in Dr. Middleton's hands, concurs nearly with
mine. As to what any one says, since it came out ; our
people (you must know,) are slow of judgement ; they
wait till some bold body saves them the trouble, and then
follow his opinion ; or stay till they hear what is said in
town, that is at some Bishop's table, or some coffee-house
about the Temple. When they are determined I will tell

you faithfully their verdict. As for *The Beauties* I am
their most humble servant. What shall I say to Mr. Lowth,
Mr. Ridley, Mr. Rolle, the Reverend Mr. Brown, Seward,
&c. ? If I say Messieurs ! this is not the thing ; write
prose, write sermons, write nothing at all ; they will
disdain me and my advice. What then would the sickly
Peer have done, that spends so much time in admiring
every thing that has four legs, and fretting at his own
misfortune in having but two ; and cursing his own politic
10 head and feeble constitution, that won't let him be such
a beast as he would wish ? Mr. S. Jenyns now and then
can write a good line or two—such as these—

> Snatch us from all our little sorrows here,
> Calm every grief, and dry each childish tear, &c.

I like Mr. Aston Hervey's Fable ; and an Ode (the last
of all) by Mr. Mason, a new acquaintance of mine, whose
Musæus too seems to carry with it a promise at least of
something good to come. I was glad to see you distinguished who poor West was, before his charming Ode, and
20 called it any thing rather than a Pindaric. The town is
an owl, if it don't like Lady Mary, and I am surprised at
it : we here are owls enough to think her eclogues very
bad ; but that I did not wonder at. Our present taste is
Sir T. Fitz-Osborne's Letters.

I send you a bit of a thing for two reasons : first, because
it is of one of your favourites, Mr. M. Green ; and next,
because I would do justice. The thought on which my
second Ode turns is manifestly stole from hence ; not
that I knew it at the time, but having seen this many
30 years before, to be sure it imprinted itself on my memory,
and, forgetting the Author, I took it for my own. The
subject was the Queen's Hermitage.

> The thinking sculpture helps to raise
> Deep thoughts, the genii of the place :

To the mind's ear, and inward sight,
There silence speaks, and shade gives light :
While insects from the threshold preach,
And minds dispos'd to musing teach ;
Proud of strong limbs and painted hues,
They perish by the slightest bruise ;
Or maladies begun within
Destroy more slow life's frail machine :
From maggot-youth, thro' change of state,
They feel like us the turns of fate :   10
Some born to creep have liv'd to fly,
And chang'd earth's cells for dwellings high :
And some that did their six wings keep,
Before they died, been forced to creep.
They politics, like ours, profess ;
The greater prey upon the less.
Some strain on foot huge loads to bring,
Some toil incessant on the wing :
Nor from their vigorous schemes desist
Till death ; and then they are never mist.   20
Some frolick, toil, marry, increase,
Are sick and well, have war and peace ;
And broke with age in half a day,
Yield to successors, and away.

*   *   *   *   *   *   *

Adieu ! I am ever yours,

T. GRAY.

XXII.

To his Mother.

Cambridge, Nov. 7, 1749.

THE unhappy news I have just received from you equally
surprizes and afflicts me. I have lost a person I loved
very much, and have been used to from my infancy ; but
am much more concerned for your loss, the circumstances 30
of which I forbear to dwell upon, as you must be too
sensible of them yourself ; and will, I fear, more and more

need a consolation that no one can give, except He who
has preserved her to you so many years, and at last, when
it was his pleasure, has taken her from us to himself : and
perhaps, if we reflect upon what she felt in this life, we
may look upon this as an instance of his goodness both to
her, and to those that loved her. She might have languished
many years before our eyes in a continual increase of pain,
and totally helpless ; she might have long wished to end
her misery without being able to attain it ; or perhaps
10 even lost all sense, and yet continued to breathe ; a sad
spectacle to such as must have felt more for her than she
could have done for herself. However you may deplore
your own loss, yet think that she is at last easy and happy ;
and has now more occasion to pity us than we her. I hope,
and beg, you will support yourself with that resignation
we owe to Him, who gave us our being for our good, and
who deprives us of it for the same reason. I would have
come to you directly, but you do not say whether you
desire I should or not ; if you do, I beg I may know it,
20 for there is nothing to hinder me, and I am in very good
health.

XXIII.

To Mr. Walpole.

Stoke, June 12, 1750.

DEAR SIR,

As I live in a place, where even the ordinary tattle of
the town arrives not till it is stale, and which produces no
events of its own, you will not desire any excuse from me
for writing so seldom, especially as of all people living
I know you are the least a friend to letters spun out of
one's own brains, with all the toil and constraint that
accompanies sentimental productions. I have been here
30 at Stoke, a few days, (where I shall continue good part of

the summer ;) and having put an end to a thing, whose beginning you have seen long ago, I immediately send it you. You will, I hope, look upon it in the light of a thing with an end to it : a merit that most of my writings have wanted, and are like to want, but which this epistle I am determined shall not want, when it tells you that I am ever

Yours,

T. GRAY.

Not that I have done yet ; but who could avoid the temptation of finishing so roundly and so cleverly, in the manner of good Queen Anne's days ? Now I have talked of writings, I have seen a book which is by this time in the press, against Middleton (though without naming him,) by Asheton. As far as I can judge from a very hasty reading, there are things in it new and ingenious, but rather too prolix, and the style here and there savouring too strongly of sermon. I imagine it will do him credit. So much for other people, now to *self* again. You are desired to tell me your opinion, if you can take the pains, of these lines. I am once more,

Ever yours.

XXIV.

To Mr. Walpole.

Cambridge, Feb. 11, 1751.

As you have brought me into a little sort of distress, you must assist me, I believe, to get out of it as well as I can. Yesterday I had the misfortune of receiving a letter from certain gentlemen (as their bookseller expresses it), who have taken the *Magazine of Magazines* into their hands : They tell me that an *ingenious* Poem, called reflections in a Country Churchyard, has been communicated to them, which they are printing forthwith ; that

they are informed that the *excellent* author of it is I by name,
and that they beg not only his *indulgence*, but the *honour*
of his correspondence, &c. As I am not at all disposed to
be either so indulgent, or so correspondent, as they desire,
I have but one bad way left to escape the honour they
would inflict upon me; and therefore am obliged to desire
you would make Dodsley print it immediately (which may
be done in less than a week's time) from your copy, but
without my name, in what form is most convenient for
10 him, but on his best paper and character; he must correct
the press himself, and print it without any interval between
the stanzas, because the sense is in some places continued
beyond them; and the title must be,—*Elegy, written in
a Country Church-yard*. If he would add a line or two to
say it came into his hands by accident, I should like it
better. If you behold the *Magazine of Magazines* in the
light that I do, you will not refuse to give yourself this
trouble on my account, which you have taken of your
own accord before now. If Dodsley do not do this immedi-
20 ately, he may as well let it alone.

XXV.

To Mr. Walpole.

Ash-Wednesday, Cambridge, 1751.

My Dear Sir, •

You have indeed conducted with great decency my little
misfortune: you have taken a paternal care of it, and
expressed much more kindness than could have been
expressed from so near a relation. But we are all frail;
and I hope to do as much for you another time.

Nurse Dodsley has given it a pinch or two in the cradle,
that (I doubt) it will bear the marks of as long as it lives.
But no matter: we have ourselves suffered under her
30 hands before now; and besides, it will only look the more

careless and by *accident* as it were. I thank you for your advertisement, which saves my honour, and in a manner *bien flatteuse pour moi*, who should be put to it even to make myself a compliment in good English.

You will take me for a mere poet, and a fetcher and carrier of sing-song, if I tell you that I intend to send you the beginning of a drama, not mine, thank God, as you will believe, when you hear it is finished, but wrote by a person whom I have a very good opinion of. It is (unfortunately) in the manner of the ancient drama, with choruses, 10 which I am to my shame the occasion of ; for, as great part of it was at first written in that form, I would not suffer him to change it to a play fit for the stage, and as he intended, because the lyric parts are the best of it, they must have been lost. The story is Saxon, and the language has a tang of Shakespear, that suits an old-fashioned fable very well. In short I don't do it merely to amuse you, but for the sake of the author, who wants a judge, and so I would lend him *mine* : yet not without your leave, lest you should have us up to dirty our stock- 20 ings at the bar of your house, for wasting the time and politics of the *nation*. Adieu, Sir !

I am ever yours,

T. GRAY.

XXVI.

To Mr. Walpole.

Stoke, Jan. 1753.

I AM at present at Stoke, to which place I came at half an hour's warning upon the news I received of my mother's illness, and did not expect to have found her alive ; but when I arrived she was much better, and continues so. I shall therefore be very glad to make you a visit at Straw-berry-hill, whenever you give me notice of a convenient 30 time. I am surprised at the print, which far surpasses my idea of London graving. The drawing itself was so finished, that I suppose it did not require all the art I had imagined to copy it tolerably. My aunts seeing me open your letter, took it to be a burying-ticket, and asked whether any body had left me a ring ; and so they still conceive it to be, even with all their spectacles on. Heaven forbid they should suspect it to belong to any verses of mine, they would burn me for a poet. On my own part I am satisfied, 10 if this design of yours succeed so well as you intend it ; and yet I know it will be accompanied with something not at all agreeable to me.—While I write this, I receive your second letter.—Sure, you are not out of your wits ! This I know, if you suffer my head to be printed, you will infallibly put me out of mine. I conjure you immediately to put a stop to any such design. Who is at the expence of engraving it, I know not ; but if it be Dodsley, I will make up the loss to him. The thing as it was, I know, will make me ridiculous enough ; but to appear in proper 20 person, at the head of my works, consisting of half a dozen ballads in thirty pages, would be worse than the pillory. I do assure you, if I had received such a book, with such a frontispiece, without any warning, I believe it would have given me a palsy. Therefore I rejoice to have received this notice, and shall not be easy till you tell me all thoughts of it are laid aside. I am extremely in earnest, and cannot bear even the idea.

I had written to Dodsley if I had not received yours, to tell him how little I liked the title which he meant to 30 prefix ; but your letter has put all that out of my head. If you think it necessary to print these explanations for the use of people that have no eyes, I should be glad they were a little altered. I am to my shame in your debt for a long letter, but I cannot think of any thing else, till you have set me at ease on this matter.

XXVII.

To Mr. Wharton.

(Extract.)

Stoke, Sept. 18, 1754.

Dear Sir,

I rejoice to find you at last settled to your heart's content, and delight to hear you talk of giving your house some *Gothic ornaments* already. If you project any thing, I hope it will be entirely within doors, and don't let me (when I come gaping into Coleman-street) be directed to the gentleman's at the ten Pinnacles, or with the church porch at his door. I am glad you enter into the spirit of Strawberry-castle ;—it has a purity and propriety of Gothicism in it, (with very few exceptions) that I have 10 not seen elsewhere. The eating-room and library were not compleated when I was there, and I want to know what effect they have. My Lord Radnor's Vagaries (I see) did not keep you from doing justice to his situation, which far surpasses every thing near it, and I do not know a more *laughing* scene, than that about Twickenham and Richmond.

I was in Northamptonshire when I received your letter, but am now returned hither. I have been at Warwick, which is a place worth seeing. The town is on an eminence, 20 surrounded every way with a fine cultivated valley, through which the Avon winds, and at the distance of five or six miles, a circle of hills well wooded, and with various objects crowning them, that close the prospect. Out of the town on one side of it, rises a rock that might remind one of your rocks at Durham, but that it is not so savage or so lofty, and that the river which washes its foot, is perfectly clear, and so gentle that its current is hardly visible. Upon it stands the castle, the noble old residence of the Beauchamps and Nevilles, and now of Earl Brooke. He 30 has sashed the great apartment that's to be sure, (I can't help these things) and being since told that square sash windows were not Gothic, he has put certain whim-whams within side the glass, which appearing through, are to look like fret-work. Then he has scooped out a little burrough in the massy walls of the place, for his little self, and his children, which is hung with paper, and printed linen, and carved chimney-pieces, in the exact manner of Berkley-square, or Argyle-buildings. What in short can a Lord do now a days, that is lost in a great old solitary Castle, but skulk about, and get into the first hole he finds, as a rat would do in like case. A pretty long old stone-bridge leads you into the town, with a mill at the end of it, over which the rock rises with the Castle upon it, with all its battlements, and queer-ruined towers, and on your left hand the Avon strays through the park, whose ancient elms seem to remember Sir Philip Sidney (who often walked under them) and talk of him to this day. The Beauchamp Earls of Warwick lie under stately monuments in the choir of the great church, and in our lady's chapel adjoining to it. There also lie Ambrose Dudley, Earl of Warwick, and his brother, the famous Lord Leicester, with Lettice, his Countess. This chapel is preserved entire, though the body of the church was burnt down sixty years ago, and rebuilt by Sir C. Wren. I had heard often of Guy-Cliff, two miles from the town, so I walked to see it ; and of all improvers commend me to Mr. Greathead, its present owner. He shewed it me himself, and is literally a fat young man, with a head and face much bigger than they are usually worn. It was naturally a very agreeable rock, whose cliffs covered with large trees hung beetling over the Avon, which twists twenty ways in sight of it ; there was the cell of Guy Earl of Warwick cut in the living stone, where he died a hermit (as you may see in a penny history, that hangs upon the rails in Moorfields) ; there were his fountains bubbling out of the cliff ;—there was a chantry founded to his memory in Henry the VIth's. time, but behold the trees are cut down to make room for flowering shrubs, the rock is cut up till it is as smooth and as sleek as satin ; the river has a gravel-walk by its side ; the cell is a grotto with cockle-shells and looking-glass; the fountains have an iron gate before them, and the chantry is a barn, or a little house. Even the poorest bits of nature that remain, are daily threatened ; for he says, (and I am sure, when the Greatheads are once set upon a thing, they will do. it) he is determined it shall be *all new*. These were his words, and they are fate. I have also been at Stow, at Woburn (the Duke of Bedford's), and at Moxton (Duke of Guilford's), but I defer these chapters till we meet. I shall only tell you for your comfort, that the parts of Northamptonshire where I have been, is in fruits, in flowers, and in corn, very near a fortnight behind this part of Buckinghamshire ; that they have no nightingales, and that the other birds are almost as silent as at Durham. It is rich land, but upon a clay, and in a very bleak, high, exposed situation. I hope you have had some warm weather, since you last complained of the south. I have thought of seeing you about Michaelmas, though I shall not stay long in town ; I should have been at Cambridge before now, if the Duke of 'Newcastle and his foundation-stone would have let me, but I want them to have done before I go. I am sorry Mr. Brown should be the only one that has stood upon punctilios with me, and would not write first ; pray tell him so. Mason is (I believe) in town, or at Chiswick. No news of Tuthill. I wrote a long letter to him in answer to one he wrote me, but no reply. Adieu !

I am ever yours,

T. G.

Brown called here this morning before I was up, and breakfasted with me.

XXVIII.

To Dr. Wharton.

Jan. 9, *Cambridge,* 1756.

DEAR DOCTOR,

I AM quite of Mr. Alderman's opinion ; provided you
have a very fair prospect of success (for I do not love
repulses, though I believe in such cases, they are not
attended with any disgrace) such an employment must
necessarily give countenance and name to one in your
profession, not to mention the use it must be of in refresh-
ing, and keeping alive the ideas of practice you have already
got, and improving them by new observation. It cannot
10 but lead to other business too, in a more natural way,
than perhaps any other, for whatever lucky chance may
have introduced into the world, here and there a Physician
of great vogue, the same chance may hardly befal another
in an age ; and the indirect and by-ways that doubtless
have succeeded with many, are rather too dirty for you to
tread. As to the time it would take up, so much the better.
Whenever it interferes with more advantageous practice, it
is in your power to quit it. In the mean time it will prepare you for that trouble and constant attendance, which
20 much business requires a much greater degree of. For
you are not to dream of being your own master, till old-
age, and a satiety of gain shall set you free. I tell you
my notions of the matter, as I see it at a distance, which
you, who stand nearer, may rectify at your pleasure.

I have continued the Soap every other day from the
time I left you, except an interval or two of a week or ten
days at a time, which I allow in order to satisfy myself,
whether the good effects of it were lasting, or only tem-
porary. I think I may say, it has absolutely cured that
30 complaint, I used to mention to you ; and (what is more)

the ill-habit, which perhaps was the cause of that, and of
the flying pains I have every now and then felt in my
joints : whenever I use it, it much increases my appetite,
and the heart-burn is quite banished, so I may venture
to say, it does good to my stomach. When I shall speak
of its bad effects, you are no longer to treat me as a whimsical body, for I am certain now that it disorders the head,
and much disturbs one's sleep. This I now avoid by taking
it immediately before dinner ; and besides these things are
trifles compared with the good it has done me. In short, 10
I am so well, it would be folly to take any other medicine,
therefore I reserve lime water, for some more pressing
occasion. I should be glad to know the particulars of
Lord Northumberland, and the Archbishop's illnesses, and
how far it has eased them in the gout.

I am glad you admire Machiavel, and are entertained
with Buffon, and edified with the divine Ashton. The
first (they say) was a good man, as much as he has been
abused ; and we will hope the best of the two latter.
Mr. [Bedingfield] who as [Lord Orford] sent me word, 20
desired to be acquainted with me, called here, before I came
down, and would pay a visit to my rooms. He made
Dr. Long conduct him thither, left me a present of a book
(not of his own writing) and a note with a very civil
compliment. I wrote to him to thank him, and have
received an answer, that fifteen years ago might have
turned my head. I know [   ] will abuse him to you,
but I insist he is a slanderer, and shall write a satire upon
him, if he does not do justice to my new admirer. I have
not added a line more to old *Caradoc*. When I do, you 30
will be sure to see it. You who give yourself the trouble
to think of my health, will not think me very troublesome,
if I beg you to bespeak me a rope-ladder (for my neighbours every day make a great progress in drunkenness,
which gives me reason to look about me) it must be full

thirty-six feet long, or a little more, but as light and manageable as may be, easy to unroll, and not likely to entangle. I never saw one, but I suppose it must have strong hooks, or something equivalent at top, to throw over an iron bar to be fixed withinside of my window. However you will chuse the properest form, and instruct me in the use of it. I see an Ephraim Hadden, near Hermitage-stairs, Wapping, that advertises them, but perhaps you may find a better artisan near you. This
10 with a canister of tea, and another of snuff, which I left at your house, and a pound of soap from Mr. Field (for mine is not so good here) will fill a box, which I beg the favour of you to send me when you can conveniently. My best compliments to Mrs. Wharton.

I am ever yours,

T. G.

XXIX.

To Mr. Mason.

Stoke, July 25, 1756.

I FEEL a contrition for my long silence ; and yet perhaps it is the last thing you trouble your head about. Nevertheless I will be as sorry as if you took it ill. I am sorry
20 too to see you so punctilious as to stand upon answers, and never to come near me till I have regularly left my name at your door, like a Mercer's Wife, that imitates people who go a visiting. I would forgive you this, if you could possibly suspect I were doing any thing that I liked better ; for then your formality might look like being piqued at my negligence, which has somewhat in it like kindness : But you know I am at Stoke, hearing, seeing, doing absolutely nothing. Not such a nothing as you do at Tunbridge, chequered and diversified with a succession of

fleeting colours ; but heavy, lifeless, without form and
void ; sometimes almost as black as the moral of Voltaire's
Lisbon, which angers you so. I have had no more muscular
inflations, and am only troubled with this depression of
mind. You will not expect therefore I should give you
any account of my *Verve*, which is at best (you know) of
so delicate a constitution, and has such weak nerves, as
not to stir out of its chamber above three days in a year.
But I shall enquire after yours, and why it is off again ?
It has certainly worse nerves than mine, if your Reviewers 10
have frighted it. Sure I (not to mention a score of your
other Critics) am something a better judge than all the
Man-Midwives and Presbyterian Parsons that ever were
born. Pray give me leave to ask you, do you find yourself
tickled with the commendations of such people ? (for you
have your share of these too) I dare say not ; your vanity
has certainly a better taste. And can then the censure
of such critics move you ? I own it is an impertinence in
these gentry to talk of one at all, either in good or in bad ;
but this we must all swallow : I mean not only we that 20
write, but all the *we's* that ever did any thing to be
talked of.

While I am writing I receive yours, and rejoice to find
that the genial influences of this fine season, which produce
nothing in me, have hatched high and unimaginable fantasies in you. I see, methinks, as I sit on Snowdon, some
glimpse of Mona and her haunted shades, and hope we
shall be very good neighbours. Any Druidical anecdotes
that I can meet with, I will be sure to send you when
I return to Cambridge ; but I cannot pretend to be learned 30
without books, or to know the Druids from modern Bishops
at this distance. I can only tell you not to go and take
Mona for the Isle of Man : it is Anglesey, a tract of plain
country, very fertile, but picturesque only from the view
it has of Caernarvonshire, from which it is separated by

the Menaï, a narrow arm of the sea. Forgive me for supposing in you such a want of erudition.

I congratulate you on our glorious successes in the Mediterranean. Shall we go in time, and hire a house together in Switzerland ? It is a fine poetical country to look at, and nobody there will understand a word we say or write.

XXX.

To Mr. Hurd.

Stoke, August 25, 1757.

I DO not know why you should thank me for what you had a right and title to ; but attribute it to the excess
10 of your politeness ; and the more so, because almost no one else has made me the same compliment. As your acquaintance in the University (you say) do me the honour to *admire*, it would be ungenerous in me not to give them notice, that they are doing a very unfashionable thing ; for all People of Condition are agreed not to admire, nor even to understand. One very great Man, writing to an acquaintance of his and mine, says that he had read them seven or eight times ; and that now, when he next sees him, he shall not have above *thirty questions* to ask. Another
20 (a Peer) believes that the last Stanza of the second Ode relates to King Charles the First and Oliver Cromwell. Even my friends tell me they do not *succeed*, and write me moving topics of consolation on that head. In short, I have heard of no body but an Actor and a Doctor of Divinity that profess their esteem for them. Oh yes, a Lady of quality, (a friend of Mason's) who is a great reader. She knew there was a compliment to Dryden, but never suspected there was any thing said about Shakespeare or Milton, till it was explained to her ; and wishes

that there had been titles prefixed to tell what they were about.

From this mention of Mason's name you may think, perhaps, we are great correspondents. No such thing; I have not heard from him these two months. I will be sure to scold in my own name, as well as in yours. I rejoice to hear you are so ripe for the press, and so voluminous; not for my own sake only, whom you flatter with the hopes of seeing your labours both public and private, but for yours too; for to be employed is to be happy. This principle of mine (and I am convinced of its truth) has, as usual, no influence on my practice. I am alone, and *ennuyé* to the last degree, yet do nothing. Indeed I have one excuse; my health (which you have so kindly enquired after) is not extraordinary, ever since I came hither. It is no great malady, but several little ones, that seem brewing no good to me. It will be a particular pleasure to me to hear whether Content dwells in Leicestershire, and how she entertains herself there. Only do not be too happy, nor forget entirely the quiet ugliness of Cambridge.

XXXI.

To Dr. Wharton.

February 21, 1758.

Dear Doctor,

I FEEL very ungrateful (which is the most uneasy of all feelings), in that I have never once enquired how you and your family enjoy the region of air and sunshine, into which you are removed, and with what contempt you look back on the perpetual fogs that hang over Mrs. Payne and Mrs. Paterson. Yet you certainly have not been the less in my mind. That at least has packed up with you, has helped Mrs. Wharton to arrange the mantle-piece, and drank tea next summer in the grotto. But I am much puzzled about the bishop and his fixtures, and do not stomach the loss of that money.

Would you know what I am doing ? I doubt you have been told already, and hold my employment cheap enough : but every one must judge of his own *capabilities*, and cut his amusements according to his disposition. The drift of my present studies, is to know, wherever I am, what
10 lies within reach, that may be worth seeing ; whether it be building, ruin, park, garden, prospect, picture, or monument. To whom it does, or has belonged, and what has been the characteristic and taste of different ages. You will say, this is the object of all antiquaries. But pray, what antiquary ever saw these objects in the same light, or desired to know them for a like reason ? In short, say what you please, I am persuaded whenever my List is finished, you will approve it, and think it of no small use. My spirits are very near the *freezing point* ; and for
20 some hours of the day, this exercise, by its warmth and gentle motion, serves to raise them a few degrees higher. I hope the misfortune that has befallen Mrs. Cibber's canary-bird will not be the ruin of *Agis*. It is probable you will have curiosity enough to see it, as it comes from the writer of *Douglas*. I expect your opinion. I am told that Swift's *History of the Tory Administration* is in the press ; and that Stuart's *Attica* will be out this spring. Adieu ! Dear Sir,

I am ever yours,

30   T. G.

Mr. Brown joins his compliments with mine to you and Mrs. Wharton.

XXXII.

To Mr. Palgrave.

Stoke, Sept. 6, 1758.

I do not know how to make you amends, having neither
rock, ruin, or precipice near me to send you ; they do not
grow in the South : but only say the word, if you would
have a compact neat box of red brick with sash windows,
or a grotto made of flints and shell-work, or a walnut-tree
with three mole-hills under it, stuck with honey-suckles
round a bason of gold-fishes, and you shall be satisfied ;
they shall come by the Edinburgh coach.

In the mean time I congratulate you on your new
acquaintance with the *savage,* the *rude,* and the *tremendous.* 10
Pray, tell me, is it any thing like what you had read in
your book, or seen in two-shilling prints ? Do not you
think a man may be the wiser (I had almost said the better)
for going a hundred or two of miles ; and that the mind
has more room in it than most people seem to think, if
you will but furnish the apartments ? I almost envy your
last month, being in a very insipid situation myself ; and
desire you would not fail to send me some furniture for
my Gothic apartment, which is very cold at present. It
will be the easier task, as you have nothing to do but 20
transcribe your little red books, if they are not rubbed
out ; for I conclude you have not trusted every thing to
memory, which is ten times worse than a lead pencil : Half
a word fixed upon or near the spot, is worth a cart-load of
recollection. When we trust to the picture that objects
draw of themselves on our mind, we deceive ourselves ;
without accurate and particular observation, it is but ill-
drawn at first, the outlines are soon blurred, the colours
every day grow fainter ; and at last, when we would

produce it to any body, we are forced to supply its defects with a few strokes of our own imagination. God forgive me, I suppose I have done so myself before now, and misled many a good body that put their trust in me. Pray, tell me, (but with permission, and without any breach of hospitality) is it so much warmer on the other side of the Swale (as some people of honour say) than it is here? Has the singing of birds, the bleating of sheep, the lowing of herds, deafened you at Rainton? Did the vaşt old
10 oaks and thick groves of Northumberland keep off the sun too much from you? I am too civil to extend my enquiries beyond Berwick. Every thing, doubtless, must improve upon you as you advanced northward. You must tell me, though, about Melross, Rosslin Chapel, and Arbroath. In short, your Port-feuille must be so full, that I only desire a loose chapter or two, and will wait for the rest till it comes out.

XXXIII.

To Mr. Mason.

Stoke, Nov. 9, 1758.

I SHOULD have told you that *Caradoc* came safe to hand; but my critical faculties have been so taken up in
20 dividing *nothing* with The Dragon of Wantley's Dam, that they are not yet composed enough for a better and more tranquil employment: shortly, however, I will make them obey me. But am I to send this copy to Mr. Hurd, or return it to you? Methinks I do not love this travelling to and again of manuscripts by the post. While I am writing, your second packet is just arrived. I can only tell you in gross, that there seem to me certain passages altered which might as well have been let alone; and

that I shall not be easily reconciled to Mador's own song. I must not have my fancy raised to that agreeable pitch of heathenism and wild magical enthusiasm, and then have you let me drop into moral philosophy and cold good sense. I remember you insulted me when I saw you last, and affected to call that which delighted my imagination, *nonsense* : Now I insist that sense is nothing in poetry, but according to the dress she wears, and the scene she appears in. If you should lead me into a superb Gothic building with a thousand clustered pillars, each of them half a mile high, the walls all covered with fretwork, and the windows full of red and blue saints that had neither head nor tail ; and I should find the Venus of Medici in person, perked up in a long niche over the high altar, do you think it would raise or damp my devotions ! I say that Mador must be entirely a Briton ; and that his preeminence among his companions must be shewn by superior wildness, more barbaric fancy, and a more striking and deeper harmony both of words and numbers : if British antiquity be too narrow, this is the place for invention ; and if it be pure invention, so much the clearer must the expression be, and so much the stronger and richer the imagery. There's for you now !

XXXIV.

To Mr. Palgrave.

London, July 24, 1759.

I AM now settled in my new territories commanding Bedford gardens, and all the fields as far as Highgate and Hampstead, with such a concourse of moving pictures as would astonish you ; so *rus-in-urbe-ish*, that I believe I shall stay here, except little excursions and vagaries, for a year to come. What though I am separated from the fashionable world by broad St. Giles's, and many a dirty court and alley, yet here is air, and sunshine, and quiet, however, to comfort you : I shall confess that I am basking with heat all the summer, and I suppose shall be blown down all the winter, besides being robbed every night ; I trust, however, that the Musæum, with all its manuscripts and rarities by the cart-load, will make ample amends for all the aforesaid inconveniences.

10 I this day past through the jaws of a great leviathan into the den of Dr. Templeman, superintendant of the reading-room, who congratulated himself on the sight of so much good company. We were, first, a man that writes for Lord Royston ; 2dly, a man that writes for Dr. Burton, of York ; 3dly, a man that writes for the Emperor of Germany, or Dr. Pocock, for he speaks the worst English I ever heard ; 4thly, Dr. Stukely, who writes for himself, the very worst person he could write for ; and, lastly, I, who only read to know if there be any thing worth 20 writing, and that not without some difficulty. I find that they printed 1000 copies of the *Harleian Catalogue*, and have sold only fourscore ; that they have £900 a year income, and spend 1300, and are building apartments for the under-keepers ; so I expect in winter to see the collection advertised and set to auction.

Have you read Lord Clarendon's Continuation of his History ? Do you remember Mr. Cambridge's account of it before it came out ? How well he recollected all the faults, and how utterly he forgot all the beauties : Surely 30 the grossest taste is better than such a sort of delicacy.

XXXV.

To Dr. Wharton.

(*Extract.*)

Southampton Row, Sept. 18, 1759.

DEAR DOCTOR,

I CANNOT say any thing to you about Mason, whose motions I am entirely a stranger to, and have not once heard from him since he left London, till (the 3d of this month) a letter came, in which he tells me, that Gaskarth is at Aston with him, and that the latter end of the month, or the beginning of the next, he shall be in town, as he goes into waiting the last fortnight in October. Lord Holdernesse has sent him no less than four expresses (literally so) with public news, good and bad, which has 10 made him of infinite importance in the eyes of that neighbourhood. I cannot pretend, therefore, to guess, whether he will be able to come to you. I am sorry to tell you, that I try in vain to execute your commission about tapestry. What is so bad as wry-mouthed histories ? and yet for this they ask me at least double the price you talk of. I have seen nothing neither, that would please me at any price. Yet I allow tapestry (if at all tolerable) to be a very proper furniture for your sort of house ; but doubt, if any bargain of that kind is to be met with, except at some old mansion- 20 sale in the country, where people will disdain tapestry, because they hear that paper is all the fashion. Stonehewer has been in Northamptonshire till now ; as you told me the subject of your letter, I did not send it thither to him, besides that, he was every day expected in town. At last he is come, and has it, but I have not yet seen him ; he is gone to day (I believe) to Portsmouth to receive a Morocco Ambassador, but returns very shortly. There is one advantage in getting into your Abbey at Christmas

time, that it will be at its worst, and if you can bear it
then, you need not fear for the rest of the year. Mr. Walpole
has lately made a new bed-chamber, which as it is in the
best taste of any thing he has yet done, and in your own
Gothic way, I must describe a little. You enter by a peaked
door at one corner of the room (out of a narrow winding
passage, you may be sure) into an alcove, in which the bed
is to stand, formed by a screen of pierced work opening
by one large arch in the middle to the rest of the chamber,
10 which is lighted at the other end by a bow-window of three
bays, whose tops are of rich painted glass in mosaic. The
cieling is covered and fretted in star and quatrefoil compartments, with roses at the intersections, all in papier
maché. The chimney on your left is the high altar in the
cathedral of Rouen (from whence the screen also is taken)
consisting of a low surbased arch between two octagon
towers, whose pinnacles almost reach the cieling, all of
nich-work ; the chairs and dressing-table are real carved
ebony, picked up at auctions. The hangings uniform,
20 purple paper, hung all over with the court of Henry
the VIII. copied after the Holbeins in the Queen's Closet
at Kensington, in black and gold frames. The bed is to
be either from Burleigh (for Lord Exeter is new-furnishing
it, and means to sell some of his original household stuff)
of the rich old tarnished embroidery ; or if that is not to
be had, and it must be new, it is to be a cut velvet with
a dark purple pattern on a stone-colour satin ground, and
deep mixed fringes and tassels. There's for you, but
I want you to see it. In the mean time I live in the Musæum,
30 and write volumes of antiquity. I have got (out of the
original Ledger-book of the Signet) King Richard the
Third's oath to Elizabeth, late *calling herself Queen of*
England, to prevail upon her to come out of sanctuary
with her five daughters ; his grant to Lady Hastings and
her son, dated six weeks after he had cut off her husband's

head; a letter to his mother; another to his chancellor, to persuade his solicitor general not to marry Jane Shore then in Ludgate by his command; Sir Thomas Wyat's Defence at his trial, when accused by Bishop Bonner of high-treason; Lady Purbeck and her son's remarkable case, and several more odd things unknown to our historians. When I come home I have a great heap of the Conway Papers (which is a secret) to read, and make out. In short, I am up to the ears.

I believe I shall go on Monday to Stoke for a time, where Lady Cobham has been dying. My best respects to Mrs. Wharton. Believe me ever

Faithfully yours,

T. G.

XXXVI.

To Dr. Clarke.

Pembroke-Hall, August 12, 1760.

NOT knowing whether you are yet returned from your sea-water, I write at random to you. For me, I am come to my resting-place, and find it very necessary, after living for a month in a house with three women that laughed from morning to night, and would allow nothing to the sulkiness of my disposition. Company and cards at home, parties by land and water abroad, and (what they call) *doing something*, that is, rackelting about from morning to night, are occupations, I find, that wear out my spirits, especially in a situation where one might sit still, and be alone with pleasure; for the place was a hill like Clifden, opening to a very extensive and diversified landscape, with the Thames, which is navigable, running at its foot.

I would wish to continue here (in a very different scene, it must be confessed) till Michaelmas; but I fear I must come to town much sooner. Cambridge is a delight of a place, now there is nobody in it. I do believe you would like it, if you knew what it was without inhabitants. It is they, I assure you, that get it an ill name and spoil all. Our friend Dr. Chapman (one of its nuisances) is not expected here again in a hurry. He is gone to his grave with five fine mackerel (large and full of roe) in his belly. He eat them all at one dinner; but his fate was a turbot on Trinity Sunday, of which he left little for the company 10 besides bones. He had not been hearty all the week; but after this sixth fish he never held up his head more, and a violent looseness carried him off.—They say he made a very good end.

Have you seen the Erse Fragments since they were printed? I am more puzzled than ever about their antiquity, though I still incline (against every body's opinion) to believe them old. Those you have already seen are the best; though there are some others that are excellent too.

XXXVII.

To Dr. Wharton.

Tuesday, [*Sept.* 8, 1761.]

20 DEAR DOCTOR,

I AM just come to town, where I shall stay six weeks, or more, and (if you will send your dimensions) will look out for papers at the shops. I own I never yet saw any Gothic papers to my fancy. There is one fault that is in the nature of the thing, and cannot be avoided. The great beauty of all Gothic designs is the variety of perspectives they occasion. This a painter may represent on the walls of a room in some measure, but not a designer of papers, where what is represented on one breadth must be exactly

repeated on another, both in the light and shade, and in
the dimensions. This we cannot help, but they do not
even do what they might. They neglect Hollar, to copy
Mr. Halfpenny's Architecture, so that all they do is more
like a goose-pie than a cathedral. You seem to suppose
that they do Gothic papers in colours, but I never saw
any but such as were to look like Stucco ; nor indeed do
I conceive that they could have any effect or meaning.
Lastly, I never saw any thing of gilding, such as you
mention, on paper ; but we shall see. Only pray leave as 10
little to my judgement as possible.

I thanked Dr. Ashton before you told me to do so. He
writes me word that (except the first Sunday of a month)
he believes he shall be at Eton, till the middle of November ;
and (as he now knows the person in question as your
nephew) adds, I remember Dr. Wharton with great pleasure,
and beg you will signify as much to him, when you write.

The King is just married ; it is the hottest night in the
year. Adieu ! it is late. I am ever

Yours, 20

T. G.

XXXVIII.

To Dr. Wharton.

Oct. 22, 1761. Southampton Row.

DEAR DOCTOR,

Do not think me very dilatory, for I have been sending
away all my things from this house (where nevertheless
I shall continue while I stay in town) and have besides
been confined with a severe cold to my room. On rum-
maging Mr. Bromwick's and several other shops, I am
forced to tell you that there are absolutely no papers at
all that deserve the name of Gothic, or that you would
bear the sight of. They are all what they call *fancy*, and 30

indeed resemble nothing that ever was in use in any age
or country. I am going to advise what perhaps you may
be deterred from by the addition of expence, but what, in
your case, I should certainly do. Anybody that can draw
the least in the world is capable of sketching in India ink
a compartment or two of diaper-work, or a niche, or
tabernacle with its fret-work. Take such a man with you
to Durham Cathedral, and let him copy one division of
any ornament you think will have any effect, from the
10 high-altar suppose, or the nine altars, or what you please.
If nothing there suits you, chuse in Dart's *Canterbury* or
Dugdale's *Warwickshire*, &c. and send the design hither.
They will execute it here, and make a new stamp on
purpose ; provided you will take twenty pieces of it, and
it will come to a halfpenny or a penny a yard, the more,
(according to the work that is in it). This I really think
worth your while. I mention your doing it there, because
it will be then under your own eye, and at your own choice,
and you can proportion the whole better to the dimensions
20 of your room : for if the design be of Arcade-work   or
any thing on a pretty large scale, and the arches, or niches,
are to rise one above another, there must be some con-
trivance that they may fill the entire space, and not be
cut in sunder and incomplete. This, indeed, where the
work is in small compartments, is not to be minded. Say,
therefore, if you come into this, or shall I take a man here
to Westminster, and let him copy some of those fret-
works ? though I think in the books that I have
named you may find better things. I much doubt of the
30 effect colours (any other than the tints of Stucco) would
have in a Gothic design on paper, and here they have
nothing to judge from. Those I spoke of at Ely were green
and pale blue, with the raised work white, if you care to
hazard it. I saw an all-silver paper quite plain, and it
looked like block-tin. In short, there is nothing I would

venture to send you. One of 3d. a yard in small compartments, might do perhaps for the stairs, but very
likely it is common, and besides it is not pure Gothic,
therefore I could not send it alone. Adieu, and tell Mason
what I shall do.

XXXIX.

To Dr. Wharton.

Nov. 13, 1761.   *London.*

DEAR DOCTOR,

I WENT as soon as I received your last letter, to chuse
papers for you at Bromwick's. I applaud your determina-
tion, for it is mere pedantry in Gothicism to stick to
nothing but Altars and Tombs, and there is no end of it, 10
if we are to sit upon nothing but Coronation-chairs, nor
drink out of nothing but chalices or flagons. The idea is
sufficiently kept up if we live in ancient houses, but with
modern conveniences about us. Nobody will expect the
inhabitants to wear ruffs and farthingales. Besides, these
things are not to be had unless we make them ourselves.

I have, however, ventured to bespeak (for the staircase)
the Stucco paper of 3d. a yard, which I mentioned to you
before. It is rather pretty, and nearly Gothic. The border
is entirely so, and where it runs horizontally, will be very 20
proper ; where perpendicularly not altogether so. I do
not see how this could be avoided. The crimson paper is
the handsomest I ever saw ; from its simplicity I believe,
as it is nothing but the same thing repeated throughout.
Mr. Trevor (Hampden) designed it for his own use ; the
border is a spiral scroll, also the prettiest I have seen. This
paper is 8d. a yard. The blue is the most extravagant :
a Mohair-flock paper of a shilling a yard, which I fear you
will blame me for : but it was so handsome, and looked

so warm, I could not resist it. The pattern is small, and will look like a cut-velvet ; the border a scroll like the last, but on a larger scale. You will ask, why the crimson (which is to be the best) is not a Mohair-paper too ? Because it would have no effect in that sort of pattern ; and it is as handsome as it need to be, without that expence. The Library paper is a cloth colour : all I can say for it is, that it was the next best design they had after the former. I think it is 7½d. a yard. They do not keep any quantity
10 by them (only samples of each sort) but promise they shall be finished in a week, and sent to your brother's, with whom I have left the bill, as I go myself to Cambridge in a day or two. Indeed, this is a very improper time to trouble him, though when I called there last night, I was told she was a great *deal better.* I did not know of his loss till you told me : on which I went to ask how they did, and found him truly in a very deplorable situation. He said he had wrote to you, but I do not know whether he was able to give you a full account of   *   *   *   *
    *   *   *   *   *   *   *

XL.

To Mr. Brown.

February 17, 1763.

20   YOU will make my best acknowledgments to Mr. Howe ; who, not content to rank me in the number of his friends, is so polite as to make excuses for having done me that honour.

I *was not born so far from the sun,* as to be ignorant of Count Algarotti's name and reputation ; nor am I so far advanced in years, or in philosophy, as not to feel the warmth of his approbation. The Odes in question, as their motto shews, were meant to be *vocal to the intelligent alone.* How few *they* were in my own country, Mr. Howe can testify ; and yet my ambition was terminated by that small circle. I have good reason to be proud, if my voice has reached the ear and apprehension of a stranger, distinguished as one of the best judges in Europe.

I am equally pleased with the just applause he bestows on Mr. Mason ; and particularly on his *Caractacus*, which is the work of a Man : whereas *Elfrida* is only that of a boy, a promising boy indeed, and of no common genius : yet this is the popular performance, and the other little known in comparison.

Neither Count Algarotti nor Mr. Howe (I believe) have heard of Ossian, the Son of Fingal. If Mr. Howe were not upon the wing, and on his way homewards, I would send it to him in Italy. He would there see that Imagination dwelt many hundred years ago, in all her pomp, on the cold and barren mountains of Scotland. The truth (I believe) is, that without any respect of climates, she reigns in all nascent societies of men, where the necessities of life, force every one to think and act much for himself.

Adieu !

XLI.

To Count Algarotti.

Cambridge, Sep. 9th, 1763.

Sir,

I received sometime since the unexpected honour of a Letter from you, and the promise of a pleasure, which till of late I had not the opportunity of enjoying. Forgive me if I make my acknowledgements in my native tongue, as I see it is perfectly familiar to you, and I (though not unacquainted with the writings of Italy) should from disuse speak its language with an ill grace, and with still more constraint to one, who possesses it in all its strength and purity.

I see with great satisfaction your efforts to reunite the congenial arts of poetry, music, and the dance, which with the assistance of painting and architecture, regulated by taste, and supported by magnificence and power, might form the noblest scene, and bestow the sublimest pleasure, that the imagination can conceive. But who shall realize these delightful visions ? There is, I own, one Prince in Europe, that wants neither the will, the spirit, nor the ability : but can he call up Milton from his grave ? can he re-animate Marcello, or bid the Barbeuna, or the Sallé move again ? can he (as much a king as he is) govern an Italian *Virtuosa*, destroy her caprice and impertinence, without hurting her talents, or command those unmeaning graces and tricks of voice to be silent, that have gained the adoration of her own country.

One cause, that so long has hindered, and (I fear) will hinder that happy union, which you propose, seems to be this : that poetry (which, as you allow, must lead the way, and direct the operation of the subordinate arts) implies at least a liberal education, a degree of literature, and various knowledge, whereas the others (with a few exceptions) are in the hands of slaves and mercenaries, I mean of people without education, who, though neither destitute of genius, nor insensible to fame, must yet make gain their principal end, and subject themselves to the prevailing taste of those, whose fortune only distinguishes them from the multitude.

I cannot help telling you, that eight or ten years ago, I was a witness to the power of your comic music.—There was a little troop of Buffi, that exhibited a Burletta in London, not in the Opera House, where the audience is chiefly of the better sort, but on one of the common Theatres full of all kinds of people, and (I believe) the fuller from that natural aversion we bear to foreigners ; their looks and their noise made it evident, they did not come thither to hear ; and on similar occasions I have known candles lighted, broken bottles, and pen knives flung on the stage, the benches torn up, the scenes hurried into the street and set on fire. The curtain drew up, the music was of Cocchi, with a few airs of Pergolesi interspersed. The singers were (as usual) deplorable, but there was one girl (she called herself the Niccolina) with little voice and less beauty ; but with the utmost justness of ear, the strongest expression of countenance, the most speaking eyes, the greatest vivacity and variety of gesture. Her first appearance instantly fixed their attention ; the tumult sunk at once, or if any murmur rose, it was hushed by a general cry for silence. Her first air ravished every body ; they forgot their prejudices, they forgot that they did not understand a word of the language ; they entered into all the humour of the part ; made her repeat all her songs, and continued their transports, their laughter, and applause to the end of the piece. Within these three last years the Paganini and Amici have met with almost the same applause once a week from a politer audience on the Opera stage. The truth is, the Opera itself, though supported here at a great expence for so many years, has rather maintained itself by the admiration bestowed on a few particular voices, on the borrowed taste of a few men of condition, that have learned in Italy how to admire, than by any genuine love we bear to the best Italian music : nor have we yet got any style of our own, and this I attribute in great measure to the language, which in spite of its energy, plenty, and the crowd of excellent writers this nation has produced, does yet (I am sorry to say it) retain too much of its barbarous original to adapt itself to musical composition. I by no means wish to have been born any thing but an Englishman ; yet I should rejoice to exchange tongues with Italy. Why this nation has made no advances hitherto in painting and sculpture it is hard to say. The fact is undeniable, and we have the vanity to apologize for ourselves, as Virgil did for the Romans, *Excudent alii, &c.* It is sure that architecture had introduced itself in the reign of the unfortunate Charles I. ,and Inigo Jones has left us some few monuments of his skill, that shew him capable of greater things. Charles had not only a love for the beautiful arts, but some taste in them. The confusion that soon followed, swept away his magnificent collection ; the artists were dispersed, or ruined, and the arts disregarded till very lately. The young monarch now on the throne is said to esteem and understand them. I wish he may have the leisure to cultivate and the skill to encourage them with due regard to merit ; otherwise it is better to neglect them. You, Sir, have pointed out the true sources, and the best examples to your countrymen ; they have nothing to do, but to be what they once were : and yet perhaps it is more difficult to restore good taste to a nation, that has degenerated, than to introduce it in one, where as yet it has never flourished. You are generous enough to wish, and sanguine enough to foresee, that it shall one day flourish in England. I too must wish, but can hardly extend my hopes so far. It is well for us that you do not see our public exhibitions.—But our artists are yet in their infancy, and therefore I will not absolutely despair.

I owe to Mr. How the honour I have of conversing with Count Algarotti, and it seems as if I meant to indulge myself in the opportunity : but I have done. Sir, I will only add, that I am proud of your approbation, having no relish for any other fame, than what is conferred by the few real judges, that are so thinly scattered over the face of the earth.

I am, Sir, with great respect,

Your most obliged humble Servant,

T. GRAY.

XLII.

To Mr. Nicholls.

Monday, 19 *Nov.,* 1764.

I RECEIVED your letter at Southampton ; and as I would
wish to treat every body, according to their own rule and
measure of good breeding, have, against my inclination,
waited till now before I answered it, purely out of fear and
respect, and an ingenuous diffidence of my own abilities.
If you will not take this as an excuse, accept it at least as
a well-turned period, which is always my principal concern.

So I proceed to tell you that my health is much improved
by the sea, not that I drank it, or bathed in it, as the
common people do : no ! I only walked by it, and looked 10
upon it. The climate is remarkably mild, even in October
and November ; no snow has been seen to lie there for•
these thirty years past ; the myrtles grow in the ground
against the houses, and Guernsey lilies bloom in every
window ; the town, clean and well-built, surrounded by
its old stone-walls, with their towers and gateways, stands
at the point of a peninsula, and opens full south to an arm
of the sea, which, having formed two beautiful bays on
each hand of it, stretches away in direct view, till it joins
the British Channel ; it is skirted on either side with 20
gently-rising grounds, cloathed with thick wood, and
directly cross its mouth rise the high lands of the Isle of
Wight at distance, but distinctly seen. In the bosom of
the woods (concealed from prophane eyes) lie hid the ruins
of Netley abbey ; there may be richer and greater houses
of religion, but the Abbot is content with his situation.
See there, at the top of that hanging meadow, under the
shade of those old trees that bend into a half circle about
it, he is walking slowly (good man !) and bidding his beads
for the souls of his benefactors, interred in that venerable 30
pile that lies beneath him. Beyond it (the meadow still

L

descending) nods a thicket of oaks that mask the building, and have excluded a view too garish and luxuriant for a holy eye ; only on either hand they leave an opening to the blue glittering sea. Did you not observe how, as that white sail shot by and was lost, he turned and crossed himself to drive the tempter from him that had thrown that distraction in his way ? I should tell you that the ferryman who rowed me, a lusty young fellow, told me that he would not for all the world pass a night at the 10 abbey (there were such things seen near it) though there was a power of money hid there. From thence I went to Salisbury, Wilton, and Stonehenge ; but of these I say no more, they will be published at the University press.

*　　*　　*　　*　　*　　*　　*

XLIII.

To Mr. Nicholls.

Pemb. Hall, August 26, 1766.

IT is long since that I heard you were gone in haste into Yorkshire on account of your mother's illness, and the same letter informed me that she was recovered, otherwise I had then wrote to you only to beg you would take care of her, and to inform you that I had discovered a thing very little known, which is, that in one's whole life one 20 can never have any more than a single mother. You may think this is obvious, and (what you call) a trite observation. You are a green gosling ! I was at the same age (very near) as wise as you, and yet I never discovered this (with full evidence and conviction I mean) till it was too late. It is thirteen years ago, and seems but as yesterday, and every day I live it sinks deeper into my heart. Many a corollary could I draw from this axiom for your use (not for my own), but I will leave you the merit of doing it for yourself. Pray tell me how your health is : I conclude 30 it perfect, as I hear you offered yourself as a guide to

Mr. Palgrave into the Sierra-Morena of Yorkshire. For
me, I passed the end of May and all June in Kent, not
disagreeably. In the west part of it, from every eminence,
the eye catches some long reach of the Thames or Medway,
with all their shipping : in the east the sea breaks in upon
you, and mixes its white transient sails and glittering
blue expanse with the deeper and brighter greens of the
woods and corn. This sentence is so fine I am quite
ashamed ; but no matter ! You must translate it into
prose. Palgrave, if he heard it, would cover his face with 10
his pudding sleeve. I do not tell you of the great and small
beasts, and creeping things innumerable, that I met with,
because you do not suspect that this world is inhabited
by any thing but men, and women, and clergy, and such
two-legged cattle. Now I am here again very disconsolate,
and all alone, for Mr. Brown is gone, and the cares of this
world are coming thick upon me : you, I hope, are better
off, riding and walking in the woods of Studley, &c. &c.
I must not wish for you here ; besides I am going to town
at Michaelmas, by no means for amusement. 20

XLIV.

To Mr. Walpole.

(Extract.)

Pembroke College, Feb. 25, 1768.

To your friendly accusation I am glad I can plead not
guilty with a safe conscience. Dodsley told me in the
Spring that the plates from Mr. Bentley's designs were
worn out, and he wanted to have them copied and reduced
to a smaller scale for a new edition. I dissuaded him from
so silly an expence, and desired he would put in no ornaments at all. The *long story* was to be totally omitted, as
its only use (that of explaining the prints) was gone : but

to supply the place of it in bulk, lest *my works* should be mistaken for the works of a flea, or a pismire, I promised to send him an equal weight of poetry or prose : so, since my return hither, I put up about two ounces of stuff, viz. the Fatal Sisters, the Descent of Odin, (of both which you have copies), a bit of something from the Welch, and certain little Notes, partly from justice (to acknowledge the debt, where I had borrowed any thing) partly from ill temper, just to tell the gentle reader that Edward I. was not Oliver Cromwell, nor Queen Elizabeth, the Witch of Endor. This is literally all ; and with all this, I shall be but a shrimp of an author. I gave leave also to print the same thing at Glasgow ; but I doubt my packet has miscarried, for I hear nothing of its arrival as yet. To what you say to me so civilly, that I ought to write more, I reply in your own words (like the Pamphleteer, who is going to confute you out of your own mouth) What has one to do when *turned of fifty*, but really to think of finishing ? However, I will be candid, (for you seem to be so with me), and avow to you, that till fourscore-and-ten, whenever the humour takes me, I will write, because I like it ; and because I like myself better when I do so. If I do not write much, it is because I cannot. As you have not this last pléa, I see no reason why you should not continue as long as it is agreeable to yourself, and to all such as have any curiosity or judgement in the subject you choose to treat. By the way let me tell you (while it is fresh) that Lord Sandwich, who was lately dining at Cambridge, speaking (as I am told) handsomely of your book, said, it was pity you did not know that his cousin Manchester had a genealogy of the Kings, which came down no lower than to Richard III. and at the end of it were two portraits of Richard and his Son, in which that King appeared to be a handsome man. I tell you it as I heard it : perhaps you may think it worth enquiring into.

Mr. Boswell's book I was going to recommend to you, when I received your letter : it has pleased and moved me strangely, all (I mean) that relates to Paoli. He is a man born two thousand years after his time ! The pamphlet proves what I have always maintained, that any fool may write a most valuable book by chance, if he will only tell us what he heard and saw with veracity. Of Mr. Boswell's truth I have not the least suspicion, because I am sure he could invent nothing of this kind. The true title of this part of his work is, a Dialogue between a Green-goose 10 and a Hero.

I have had certain observations on your Royal and Noble Authors given me to send you perhaps about three years ago : last week I found them in a drawer, and (my conscience being troubled) now enclose them to you. I have even forgot whose they are.

I have been also told of a passage in Ph. de Comines, which (if you know) ought not to have been passed over. The Book is not at hand at present, and I must conclude my letter. 20

Adieu ! I am ever yours,

T. GRAY.

XLV.

To Dr. Wharton.

Jermyn Street, Aug. 1, (*at Mr. Roberts's*) 1768.

DEAR DOCTOR,

I HAVE been remiss in answering your last letter, which was sent me to Ramsgate, from Cambridge. For I have passed a good part of the summer in different parts of Kent, much to my satisfaction. Could I have advised any thing essential in poor Mrs. —— case, I had certainly replied immediately, but we seem of one mind in it. There was nothing left but to appeal to delegates (let the trouble 30 and expense be what they will almost) and to punish, if it be practicable, that old villain, who upon the bench of justice dared to set at nought all common sense and humanity.

I write to you now chiefly to tell you (and I think you will be pleased, nay I expect the whole family will be pleased with it) that on Sunday se'nnight, Brocket, died by a fall from his horse, being (as I hear) drunk, and some say, returning from Hinchinbroke. That on the Wednesday
10 following I received a letter from the D. of Grafton, saying he had the king's commands to *offer* me the vacant Professorship, that, &c. (but I shall not write all he says) and he adds at the end, *that from private as well as public considerations, he must take the warmest part in approving so well judged a measure, as he hopes I do not doubt of the real regard and esteem with which he has the honor to be,* &c. there's for you, so on Thursday the king signed the warrant, and next·day at his levée I kissed his hand ; he made me several gracious speeches ; which I shall not report, because
20 every body who goes to Court, does so. By the way, I desire you would say, that all the Cabinet Council in words of great favour approved the nomination of your humble servant : and this I am bid to say, and was told to leave my name at their several doors. I have told you the outside of the matter, and all the manner. For the inside you know enough easily to guess it, and you will guess right. As to his grace I have not seen him before or since.

I shall continue here perhaps a fortnight longer, perishing
30 with heat ; I have no Thermometer with me, but I feel it as I did at Naples. Next summer (if it be as much in my power, as it is in my wishes) I meet you at the foot of Skiddaw. My respects to Mrs. Wharton, and the young ladies great and small. Love to Robin and Richard. Adieu !

I am truly yours.

XLVI.

To Mr. Nicholls.

(Extract.)

Pembroke College, June 24, 1769.

AND so you have a garden of your own, and you plant
and transplant, and are dirty and amused ! Are not you
ashamed of yourself ? Why, I have no such thing, you
monster, nor ever shall be either dirty or amused as long
as I live. My gardens are in the windows like those of
a lodger up three pair of stairs in Petticoat Lane, or Camo-
mile Street, and they go to bed regularly under the same
roof that I do. Dear, how charming it must be to walk
out in one's own *garding*, and sit on a bench in the open
air, with a fountain and leaden statue, and a rolling stone, 10
and an arbour : have a care of sore throats though, and
the *agoe.*

Odicle has been rehearsed again and again, and the
scholars have got scraps by heart : I expect to see it torn
piece-meal in the *North Briton* before it is born. If you
will come you shall see it, and sing in it amidst a chorus
from Salisbury and Gloucéster music meeting, great names
there, and all well versed in *Judas Maccabæus.* I wish it
were once over ; for then I immediately go for a few days
to London, and so with Mr. Brown to Aston, though I fear 20
it will rain the whole summer, and Skiddaw will be invisible
and inaccessible to mortals.

I have got De la Lande's *Voyage through Italy,* in eight
volumes ; he is a member of the academy of sciences, and
pretty good to read. I have read too an octavo volume of
Shenstone's *Letters* : Poor Man ! he was always wishing
for money, for fame, and other distinctions ; and his whole
philosophy consisted in living against his will in retire-

ment, and in a place which his taste had adorned ; but which he only enjoyed when people of note came to see and commend it : his correspondence is about nothing else but this place and his own writings, with two or three neighbouring clergymen who wrote verses too.   *   *   *

I have just found the beginning of a letter, which somebody had dropped : I should rather call it first thoughts for the beginning of a letter ; for there are many scratches and corrections. As I cannot use it myself (having got
10 a beginning already of my own) I send it for your use on some great occasion.

>   *Dear Sir,*
>   " After so long silence, the hopes of pardon, and prospect
> " of forgiveness might seem entirely extinct, or at least
> " very remote, was I not truly sensible of your goodness
> " and candour, which is the only asylum that my negligence
> " can fly to, since every apology would prove insufficient
> " to counter-balance it, or alleviate my fault : How then
> " shall my deficiency presume to make so bold an attempt,
> 20 " or be able to suffer the hardships of so rough a cam-
> " paign ? &c. &c. &c.

Journal, 1769.

(*To Dr. Wharton.*)

October 3. Wind at S. E. ; a heavenly day. Rose at 7, and walked out under the conduct of my landlord to *Borrodale.* The grass was covered with a hoar frost, which soon melted and exhaled in a thin blueish smoke. Crossed the meadows obliquely, catching a diversity of views among the hills over the lake and islands, and changing prospect at every ten paces ; left *Cockshut* and *Castle-hill* (which we formerly mounted) behind me, and drew near the foot of *Walla-crag*, whose bare and rocky brow, cut perpendicularly down above 400 feet, as I guess, awefully overlooks the way ; our path here tends to the left, and the ground gently rising, and covered with a glade of scattering trees and bushes on the very margin of the water, opens both ways the most delicious view, that my eyes ever beheld. Behind you are the magnificent heights of *Walla-crag* ; opposite lie the thick hanging woods of Lord Egremont, and *Newland* valley, with green and smiling fields embosomed in the dark cliffs ; to the left the 10 jaws of *Borrodale*, with that turbulent chaos of mountain behind mountain, rolled in confusion ; beneath you, and stretching far away to the right, the shining purity of the *Lake*, just ruffled by the breeze, enough to shew it is alive, reflecting rocks, woods, fields, and inverted tops of mountains, with the white buildings of *Keswick*, *Crosthwait* church, and *Skiddaw* for a back ground at a distance. Oh ! Doctor ! I never wished more for you ; and pray think how the glass played its part in such a spot, which is called Carf-close-reeds ; I chuse to set down these 20 barbarous names, that any body may enquire on the place, and easily find the particular station that I mean. This scene continues to *Barrow-gate* ; and a little farther, passing a brook called *Barrow-beck*, we entered *Borrodale*. The crags, named *Lodoor-banks*, now begin to impend terribly over your way ; and more terribly when you hear, that three years since an immense mass of rock tumbled at once from the brow, and barred all access to the dale (for this is the only road) till they could work their way through it. Luckily no one was passing at the 30 time of this fall ; but down the side of the mountain, and far into the lake, lie dispersed the huge fragments of this ruin, in all shapes and in all directions. Something farther, we turned aside into a coppice, ascending a little in front of *Lodoor* water-fall, the height appears to be about 200 feet,

the quantity of water not great, though (these three days
excepted) it had rained daily in the hills for near two
months before ; but then the stream was nobly broken,
leaping from rock to rock, and foaming with fury. On
one side a towering crag, that spired up to equal, if not
overtop, the neighbouring cliffs (this lay all in shade and
darkness) ; on the other hand a rounder broader projecting
hill, shagged with wood, and illumined by the sun, which
glanced sideways on the upper part of the cataract. The
10 force of the water wearing a deep channel in the ground,
hurries away to join the lake. We descended again, and
passed the stream over a rude bridge. Soon after we came
under *Gowder* crag, a hill more formidable to the eye and
to the apprehension than that of *Lodoor* ; the rocks a-top,
deep-cloven, perpendicularly, by the rains, hanging loose
and nodding forwards, seem just starting from their base
in shivers ; the whole way down, and the road on both
sides, is strewed with piles of the fragments, strangely
thrown across each other, and of a dreadful bulk. The
20 place reminds one of those passes in the Alps, where the
guides tell you to move on with speed and say nothing,
lest the agitation of the air should loosen the snows above,
and bring down a mass that would overwhelm a caravan.
I took their counsel here and hastened on in silence.

Non ragioniam di lor ; ma guarda, e passa !

October 3. The hills here are clothed all up their steep
sides with oak, ash, birch, holly, &c. : some of it has been
cut 40 years ago, some within these eight years, yet all is
sprung again green, flourishing, and tall for its age, in
30 a place where no soil appears but the staring rock, and
where a man could scarce stand upright.

Met a civil young farmer overseeing his reapers (for it is
oat-harvest here) who conducted us to a neat white house
in the village of Grange, which is built on a rising ground

in the midst of a valley. Round it the mountains form an awful amphitheatre, and through it obliquely runs the Derwent clear as glass, and shewing under its bridge every trout that passes. Beside the village rises a round eminence of rock, covered entirely with old trees, and over that more proudly towers Castle-crag, invested also with wood on its sides, and bearing on its naked top some traces of a fort said to be Roman. By the side of the hill, which almost blocks up the way, the valley turns to the left and contracts its dimensions, till there is hardly any road but the rocky bed of the river. The wood of the mountain increases, and their summits grow loftier to the eye, and of more fantastic forms : among them appear *Eagle's-Cliff*, *Dove's-Nest*, *Whitedale-pike*, &c. celebrated names in the annals of Keswick. The dale opens about four miles higher till you come to *Sea-Whaite* (where lies the way mounting the hills to the right, that leads to the *Wadd-mines*) : all farther access is here barred to prying mortals, only there is a little path winding over the Fells, and for some weeks in the year passable to the Dale's-men ; but the mountains know well that these innocent people will not reveal the mysteries of their ancient kingdom, the reign of Chaos and Old Night : only I learned that this dreadful road, dividing again, leads one branch to *Ravenglas*, and the other to *Hawkshead*.

For me, I went no farther than the farmer's at *Grange :* his mother and he brought us butter, that Siserah would have jumped at, though not in a lordly dish, bowls of milk, thin oaten cakes and ale ; and we had carried a cold tongue thither with us. Our farmer was himself the man, that last year plundered the eagle's eirie : all the dale are up in arms on such an occasion, for they lose abundance of lambs yearly, not to mention hares, partridges, grouse, &c. He was let down from the cliff in ropes to the shelf of rock, on which the nest was built, the people above shouting and holloaing to fright the old birds, which flew screaming round, but did not dare to attack him. He brought off the eaglet (for there is rarely more than one) and an addle egg. The nest was roundish and more than a yard over, made of twigs twisted together. Seldom a year passes but they take the brood or eggs, and sometimes they shoot one, sometimes the other parent, but the survivor has always found a mate (probably in Ireland), and they breed near the old place. By his description I learn, that this species is the *Erne* (the Vultur *Albicilla* of Linnæus in his last edition, but in yours *Falco Albicilla*) so consult him and Pennant about it.

Walked leisurely home the way we came, but saw a new landscape : the features indeed were the same in part, but many new ones were disclosed by the mid-day sun, and the tints were entirely changed. Take notice this was the best or perhaps the only day for going up Skiddaw, but I thought it better employed : it was perfectly serene, and hot as Midsummer. In the evening walked alone down to the Lake by the side of *Crow-Park* after sun-set, and saw the solemn colouring of light draw on, the last gleam of sunshine fading away on the hilltops, the deep serene of the waters, and the long shadows of the mountains thrown across them, till they nearly touched the hithermost shore. At distance heard the murmur of many waterfalls, not audible in the day-time. Wished for the Moon, but she was *dark to me and silent, hid in her vacant interlunar cave.*

NOTES

PAGE **1**, l. 21. *at Florence.* ' Dr. Johnson has two slight mistakes in his *Life of Gray.* He says that they quarrelled at Florence and parted, instead of Reggio. He says also that Gray began his poem *De Principiis Cogitandi* after his return ; but it was commenced in the winter of 1740, at Florence.' (Mitford.)

PAGE **7**, l. 33. *a fantastic foppery.* In a letter to Wharton, Gray says : ' I by no means pretend to inspiration, but yet I affirm that the faculty in question is by no means voluntary. It is the result (I suppose) of a certain disposition of mind, which does not depend on one's self, and which I have not felt this long time.' (June 18, 1758.) Compare Letter XXIX.

PAGE **8**, l. 31. *His supplication to Father Thames.* Are we by this rule of criticism to judge the following passage, in the twentieth chapter of *Rasselas* ? ' As they were sitting together, the princess cast her eyes upon the river that flowed before her : " *Answer* ", said she, " *great Father of Waters,* thou that rollest thy floods through eighty nations, *to the invocation* of the daughter of thy native king. *Tell me if thou waterest,* through all thy course, a single habitation, from which thou dost not hear the murmurs of complaint." ' (Mitford.)

For the charge of obscurity see Letter XXX, and the note on the extract from Cowper's correspondence, p. 17.

James Beattie, LL.D. (1735–1803), Professor of Moral Philosophy and Logic at Aberdeen, was author of several philosophical works and of some minor verse, of which ' The Minstrel ' is the best. He was an admirer of Gray, and made his acquaintance in 1765 when Gray was on his Scottish tour. His opinion of the ' Elegy ' is expressed in a letter to Lady Forbes of 12 October 1772 :

. . . ' Again your ladyship must have observed that some sentiments are common to all men ; others peculiar to persons of a certain character. Of the former sort are those which Gray has so elegantly expressed in his " Church-yard Elegy ", a poem which is universally understood and admired, not only for its poetical beauties, but also, and perhaps chiefly, for its expressing sentiments in which every man thinks himself interested, and which, at certain times, are familiar to all men. Now the sentiments expressed in " The Minstrel " being not common to all men, but peculiar to persons of a certain cast, cannot possibly be interesting, because the generality of readers will not understand nor feel them so thoroughly as to think them natural.' (*Life of Beattie* by Sir William Forbes, ed. 1807, i. 265–6.)

COWPER

PAGE **17,** l. 22. *Sublime* : Burke had fixed the meaning of the word for his generation. ' Whatever is fitted in any sort to excite the ideas of pain and danger, that is to say, whatever is in any sort terrible, or is conversant about terrible objects, or operates in a manner analogous to terror, is a source of the *sublime*. . . . A level plain of a vast extent on land is certainly no mean idea ; the prospect of such a plain may be as extensive as a prospect of the ocean : but can it ever fill the mind with anything so great as the ocean itself ? This is owing to several causes ; but it is owing to none more than this, that this ocean is an object of no small terror. Indeed terror is in all cases whatsoever, either more openly or latently, the ruling principle of the sublime.'

This led him to defend ' obscurity ' as a legitimate device in art. ' To make anything very terrible, obscurity seems in general to be necessary. When we know the full extent of any danger, when we can accustom our eyes to it, a great deal of the apprehension vanishes. Every one will be sensible of this who considers how greatly night adds to our dread, in all cases of danger, and how much the notions of ghosts and goblins, of which none can form clear ideas, affect minds which give credit to the popular tales. . . . No person seems better to have understood the secret of heightening, or of setting terrible things, if I may use the expression, in their strongest light, by the force of a judicious obscurity, than Milton. His description of Death in the second book is admirably studied, . . . all is dark, uncertain, confused, terrible, and sublime to the last degree.' (*The Sublime and Beautiful*, 1757, i. 7, ii. 2, 3.)

PAGE **17,** l. 24. *Thursday society* : ' The Nonsense Club ', a society of literary triflers, all Westminster scholars and students of the Temple.

NOTES ON THE POEMS

PAGE 32. ODE ON THE SPRING. Gray wrote this poem in June 1742, and sent it to his friend West, ' not knowing ', as he says, ' he was then dead '. It was published in 1748.

l. 2. *Venus' train*. The ' Hours ' were associated with Aphrodite both by Homer and by Hesiod.

l. 4. *purple year* : so Pope in his first Pastoral, l. 28 :

And lavish Nature paints the purple year.

l. 5. *The Attic warbler* : the nightingale. Gray combines Milton's

The Attic bird trills her thick warbled notes.

(*Paradise Lost*, iv. 245.)

and Pope's

Is it for thee the linnet pours her throat.

(*Essay on Man*, iii. 33.)

l. 25. *The insect youth*. For Gray's debt to Matthew Green in this passage, see Letter XXV. ' He congratulated himself on not having a good verbal memory,' says Nicholls, ' for without it he said he had imitated too much ; and if he had possessed such a memory, all that he wrote would have been imitation.' (*Reminiscences* of Gray.)

PAGE 34. ODE ON THE DEATH OF A FAVOURITE CAT : See Letter XX. After Gray's death Walpole placed the bowl on a pedestal at Strawberry-hill, with the first four lines of this Ode for an inscription : reading

'Twas on *this* vase's lofty side, &c.

l. 3. *The azure flowers*. See Johnson's remarks, p. 8.

l. 16. *Tyrian hue* : i. e. the royal purple, obtained in antiquity from a shell-fish, the murex, found near Tyre.

l. 34. *No Dolphin came* : alluding to the story of Arion, the harper, who was thrown into the sea and saved by a dolphin charmed by his music.

PAGE 35. ODE ON A DISTANT PROSPECT OF ETON COLLEGE. The first of Gray's poems to be printed (1747). It was written at Stoke Poges in 1742 during the depression caused by the death of his friend West, and by his quarrel with Walpole and Ashton.

l. 4. *Henry's* : King Henry VI, founder of the College.

l. 29. *the rolling circle's speed.* Gray originally wrote ' the hoop's elusive speed ', but clearly felt that ' hoop ' was a word too low for poetry. Compare Cowper's apologies for calling a cucumber a cucumber (*Task*, iii. 446). Wordsworth must have been thinking of such devices when he began his sonnet :

Spade ! with which Wilkinson hath tilled his lands.

PAGE **39**. HYMN TO ADVERSITY. Written in 1742, published in 1753.

l. 35. *Gorgon terrors.* Compare Milton (*P.L.* ii. 611), ' Medusa with Gorgonian terror ' : allusions to the myth of the snake-haired Medusa, whose appearance had power to turn the spectator to stone. Perseus, who slew her, escaped this fate by looking only at her reflection in his shield.

PAGE **41**. THE PROGRESS OF POESY. Written at Cambridge in 1754 ; first published with ' The Bard ' in 1757, without notes. ' It appeared ', says Wharton, ' that there were not twenty people in England who liked them.' Piqued by the charge of obscurity (see Letter XXX) Gray added notes in the edition of 1768, with the following explanation : ' When the author first published this and the following Ode he was advised, even by his friends, to subjoin some explanatory notes ; but had too much respect for the understanding of his readers to take that liberty.'

The Motto may be translated : ' Vocal to the intelligent, but for the world at large requiring interpreters.'

l. 1. *Æolian lyre* : alluding to Æolia, in Asia Minor, the district which produced Alcaeus and Sappho.

l. 17. *Thracia's hills.* Ares, the god of war, was associated with Thrace, the ferocity of whose inhabitants was for a time tamed by the songs of Orpheus.

ll. 27, 29. *Idalia . . . Cytherea.* Aphrodite was associated with the island of Cythera, but was worshipped also at Idalion in Cyprus.

l. 27. *velvet-green.* Johnson's objection seems to be two-fold ; first, that ' a metaphor from art degrades nature ', and secondly, that the compound is ' cant ', i. e. slang or jargon. Perhaps it reminded him of terms used in the drapery trade. In the fashion columns of the *Ladies' Magazine* a little later I find references to ' flame-of-burnt-brandy blue ', ' French Pomona-green ', ' marble-dust grey ', ' broad Cleopatra-backs ', and ' style-of-Isis ringlets '.

l. 35. *many-twinkling* : another awkward compound (see Johnson), formed by analogy with Greek. Gray means that they were ' many ' and that they were ' twinkling ' ; but with characteristic over subtlety he fabricates a compound in which 'many' must have an adverbial value (i. e. ' many-ly ', or ' in a many fashion '). He is trying to suggest the appearance of the dancers' white feet, which move so swiftly that they seem more numerous than they are. But the English language will not allow of the device which he adopts. Johnson's objection is unanswerable.

l. 53. *Hyperion* : Ruler of the sun during the reign of the Titans, before the gods were. Gray follows Shakespeare (*Hamlet*, I. ii), and was followed by Keats in a false quantity. The name is Hyperion.

l. 66. *Delphi* : the centre of the cult of Apollo.

l. 68. *Ilissus* : the river of Athens.

l. 69. *Mæander* : a river of Asia Minor.

l. 77. *the sad Nine* : the Muses.

l. 78. *Latian plains* : Italy.

l. 86. *the mighty Mother* : Nature.

l. 102. *closed his eyes in endless night.* ' Nothing was ever more violently distorted than this material fact of Milton's blindness having been occasioned by his intemperate studies and late hours during his prosecution of the defence against Salmasius—applied to the dazzling effects of too much mental vision. His corporal sight was blasted with corporal occupation ; his inward sight was not impaired but rather strengthened by his task. If his course of studies had turned his brain, there would have been some fitness in the expression.' (Charles Lamb in *The London Magazine*, December 1822.)

A prosaic criticism, unworthy of Lamb. Compare Alaric Watts on Wordsworth's ' The Daffodils ': ' the single idea is that of a bed of daffodils " dancing " in the breeze. As however the root of the flower remains without motion, it cannot be said to " dance ". The image is a false one.'

PAGE **47**. THE BARD. Begun in 1754, laid aside in 1755, and completed in 1757 for publication with ' The Progress of Poesy '.

' The Bard ' was Gray's first excursion into Mediaevalism. None of his notes cite parallels from classical writers.

l. 18. *haggard* : ' a metaphor taken from an unreclaimed Hawk, which is called a Haggard, and looks wild and *farouche*, and jealous of its liberty.' (Gray to Wharton, 21 Aug. 1755.)

l. 20. ' The beard of Gray's Bard, " streaming like a meteor ", had always struck me as an injudicious imitation of the Satanic ensign in *Paradise Lost*, which

full high advanced
Shone like a meteor streaming to the wind,

till the other day I met with a passage in Heywood's old play, *The Four Prentices of London*, which it is difficult to imagine

not to be the origin of the similitude in both poets.   The
line in italics Gray has almost verbatim adopted—

> In Sion towers hangs his victorious flag,
> Blowing defiance this way ; and it shows
> *Like a red meteor in the troubled air,*
> Or like a blazing comet that foretells
> The fall of princes.

All is here noble, and as it should be.   The comparison enlarges
the thing compared without stretching it upon a violent rack
till it bursts with ridiculous explosion.   The application of
such gorgeous imagery to an old man's beard is of a piece
with the Bardolphian bombast : " see you these meteors,
these exhalations ? " or the raptures of an Oriental lover who
should compare his mistress's nose to a watch-tower or a
steeple.' (Charles Lamb in *The Examiner*, 12 September 1813.)

l. 28.   *Hoel* and *Llewellyn* : Welsh bards and princes.

l. 29.   *Cadwallo, Urien, Modred* : Welsh bards.

l. 49.   *Weave the warp*, &c. See Johnson's criticism, p. 12.
' Mrs. Thrale maintained that his Odes were melodious ;
upon which he exclaimed,

> Weave the warp, and weave the woof.

I added, in a solemn tone,

> The winding sheet of Edward's race.

" *There* is a good line." " Ay," said he, " and the next line
is a good one (pronouncing it contemptuously) :

> Give ample verge and room enough.

No, Sir, there are but two good stanzas in Gray's poetry,
which are in his *Elegy in a Country Churchyard.*" He then
repeated the stanza,

> For who to dumb forgetfulness a prey, &c.

mistaking one word ; for instead of *precincts* he said *confines.*
He added, " The other stanza I forget." ' (Boswell, 28 March
1775.)

l. 52.   *characters* : i. e. letters, in the original sense.

l. 53.   *mark the year* : the 21st of September 1327, when
Edward II was murdered in Berkeley Castle by Gournay and
Ogle.

PAGE **54.** THE FATAL SISTERS. This and the following two
poems replaced ' The Long Story ' in the volume of Gray's
Works of 1768. ' This poem is not so much a translation, as
a loose, though highly spirited paraphrase.' (Mitford.) Gray
depended chiefly on the Latin translation of the Icelandic poem,
contained in the *Orcades* of Thormodus Forfaeus, 1697.

l. 44.   *a King* : Sictryg.

l. 45.   *Eirin* : Ireland.

PAGE 57. THE DESCENT OF ODIN. See note on the previous poem. The original is to be found in Saemund's *Edda*, but Gray used the Latin translation of Bartholinus in his *De Causis contemnendae Mortis*, 1689. ' Gray translated only that part of it which he found in the Latin version of Bartholinus ; and to this cause much of the obscurity is owing.' (Mitford.)

It was revealed to Balder (the summer sun-god) that he must die. To avert this fate his mother Frigg, the Earth goddess, sent her maidservants to take oaths from all living creatures, herbs, minerals, and stones not to do any hurt to Balder. Only the mistletoe was so slender and weak that of it no oath was demanded. And Frigg rejoiced, thinking that her son was safe. But his father Odin was not satisfied. He mounted his horse, Sleipnir, and rode down past Nifl-hel (Hell) and the Hell-hound, Garm (l. 5), to Hela (Elysium), where the souls of the righteous dwell. There also is the dwelling of the Asmegir, who are to be rulers of a new Heaven and a new Earth, when Odin and his world have passed away. The Asmegir were already preparing to welcome Balder, for they desired that he should be their ruler until the dawn of the world's new age.

Odin rode to the eastern gate, where he knew there was the grave of a great prophetess, and by his spells raised her from the dead to answer his questions, concealing his godship under the name of Vegtam. She told him that the preparations of the Asmegir (ll. 41–6) were indeed for Balder, who must die ; that his slayer should be his brother, blind Hodur (Night or Winter) ; and that he should be avenged by Vale (the May-god), who should be the son of Odin by Rhind, the snow-goddess (l. 65).

All this was afterwards accomplished. While the gods in their sport were hurling javelins at Balder and smiting him with their swords, the evil one, Loke, caused an arrow to be made of mistletoe, which he gave to Hodur ; and with the arrow Hodur unwittingly slew Balder. Straightway a messenger was sent to Urd, the Queen of Hela, beseeching her that Balder might return ; but her answer was that it might not be unless all living things should weep for him. Then Frigg sent to beseech all living things to weep ; but the hag Angerboda (Darkness, the mother of evil monsters) would not weep, and Balder was lost to them for ever. (In the poem Odin suddenly reveals himself as a god by his fore-knowledge of this episode of the weeping, and denounces the prophetess as the evil Angerboda herself, ll. 75–86.)

For the part that he played in the tragedy Loke was bound upon a three-edged rock (l. 90), and there he lies in torment till the Twilight of the Gods, when he will join the giants and the powers of evil in their last assault upon Heaven, and die by the hand of Heimdal, sentinel of Heaven's bridge.

PAGE 60. THE TRIUMPHS OF OWEN. See note on the Fatal Sisters. The original Welsh of the above poem was the composition of Gwalchmai, the son of Melir, immediately after Prince Owen Gwynedd had defeated the combined fleets of Iceland, Denmark, and Norway, which had invaded his territory on the coast of Anglesea. The battle was fought in the year 1157. 'It seems' (says Dr. Evans, *Specimens of Welsh Poetry*, 1764) ' that the fleet landed in some part of the frith of Menai, and that it was a kind of mixt engagement, some fighting from the shore, others from the ships ; and probably the great slaughter was owing to its being low-water, and that they could not sail.' Gray depended upon Evans's *Specimens*. (Mitford.)

l. 4. *Gwyneth* : North Wales.

l. 14. *Lochlin* : Denmark.

l. 20. *The Dragon-Son*: 'The red dragon is the device of Cadwallader, which all his descendants bore on their banners.' (Mason.)

PAGE 62. ELEGY WRITTEN IN A COUNTRY CHURCHYARD. Begun possibly in 1742, but more probably in 1746 at Stoke Poges, and perhaps carried as far as l. 72, with the four stanzas preserved by Mason, as its conclusion (see note at l. 72). Revised and completed in 1749–50, and sent to Walpole (see Letter XXII). It was circulated in manuscript copies until the editor of *The Magazine of Magazines* applied to Gray for leave to publish it ; whereupon Gray got it published by Dodsley without his name (see Letter XXIII). ' It went through four editions in two months,' Gray noted, ' and afterwards a fifth, sixth, seventh, eighth, ninth, tenth, and eleventh ; printed also in 1753 with Mr. Bentley's Designs, of which there is a second edition ; and again by Dodsley in his Miscellany, vol. iv, and in a Scotch Collection call'd *The Union* ; translated into Latin by Chr. Anstey, Esq., and the Rev. Mr. Roberts, and published in 1762, and again in the same year by Rob. Lloyd, M.A.' It had the success of a popular ballad. General Wolfe is said to have declaimed it to his officers on the eve of the battle of Quebec, and to have added: ' I would prefer being the author of that Poem to the glory of beating the French tomorrow.' It was translated into the chief European languages, and had a considerable vogue in France owing to the republican sentiment which it was supposed to contain. Marie-Joseph Chénier published a translation of it in 1805 to supersede the paraphrases and imitations which had done duty for it in French. Gray told Dr. Gregory ' with a good deal of acrimony ' that it ' owed its popularity entirely to the subject, and that the public would have received it as well

if it had been written in prose '. But in that he was clearly
mistaken. It is evident from the swarm of imitations or
unconscious echoes which it produced in contemporary poetry
that it had charmed the age by its metrical splendour and
verbal music quite as much as by its sentiment.

l. 2. *wind* : ' herd ', as a collective noun, may be allowed
the plural.

l. 35. *awaits* : the subject of the verb is the ' hour '. The
inversion is not very happy. No one can read the stanza
without feeling that ' The boast of heraldry ', &c., should be
in the nominative case. Rhetoric seems to demand it. But
Gray was thinking in Latin.

l. 35. *th' inevitable hour* : a subconscious recollection of
his friend West's ' Monody on the Death of Queen Caroline ' :

> Ah me ! what boots us all our boasted power,
> Our golden treasure and our purple state ?
> They cannot ward the inevitable hour,
> Nor stay the fearful violence of fate.

l. 39. *fretted*: adorned with interlacing fillets. Cf. *Hamlet*,
II. ii, ' this Majesticall Roofe, fretted with golden fire.'

l. 41. *storied* : probably ' bearing an inscription ' ; a rather
awkward adaptation of Milton's coinage (*Il Penseroso*, 159) :

> And storied windows richly dight,

where it means ' painted with stories, that is, histories '.
animated : life-like.

ll. 45–8. ' There has always appeared to me a vicious
mixture of the figurative with the real in this admired passage.
The first two lines may barely pass, as not bad. But the
hands laid in the earth must mean the identical five-fingered
organs of the body ; and how does this consist with their
occupation of *swaying rods*, unless their owner had been
a schoolmaster ; or *waking lyres*, unless he were literally a
harper by profession ? Hands that " might have held the
plough " would have some sense, for that work is strictly
manual ; the others only emblematically or pictorially so.
Kings nowadays sway no rods, *alias* sceptres, except on their
coronation day ; and poets do not necessarily strum upon the
harp or fiddle as poets.' (Charles Lamb in *The London
Magazine*, December 1822.)

But much good poetry would be destroyed by this criticism : e. g.

> Or whether thou to our moist vows deny'd,
> Sleep'st by the fable of Bellerus old. (*Lycidas*, 159.)

The body of a dead man (' this identical ' four-limbed structure
of flesh and bone) cannot be said to ' sleep by ' a ' fable ',

except figuratively. Yet the beauty of the passage depends upon this ' mixture of the figurative with the real ' ; suggesting, as it does, that the young man whom they all knew is already numbered with the heroes of half-remembered myth.

ll. 57–60. From the original manuscript, now preserved at Eton College, it appears that for Hampden he first wrote ' Cato ', for Milton ' Tully ', and for Cromwell ' Caesar '. His second thoughts were, as usual, an improvement.

l. 61. ' Edwards, the author of *The Canons of Criticism*, here added the two following stanzas, to supply what he deemed a defect in the poem ' (Mitford) :

> Some lovely Fair, whose unaffected charms
>   Shone with attraction to herself unknown :
> Whose beauty might have bless'd a Monarch's arms,
>   Whose virtue cast a lustre on a throne.

> That humble beauty warm'd an honest heart,
>   And cheer'd the labours of a faithful spouse ;
> That virtue form'd for every decent part
>   The healthful offspring that adorn'd their house.

l. 72. After this verse, in the original manuscript of the poem, are the four following stanzas :

> The thoughtless World to Majesty may bow
>   Exalt the brave, & idolize Success
> But more to Innocence their Safety owe
>   Than Power & Genius e'er conspired to bless

> And thou, who mindful of the unhonour'd Dead
>   Dost in these Notes their artless Tale relate
> By Night & lonely Contemplation led
>   To linger in the gloomy Walks of Fate

> Hark how the sacred Calm, that broods around
>   Bids ev'ry fierce tumultuous Passion cease
> In still small Accents whisp'ring from the Ground
>   A grateful Earnest of eternal Peace

> No more with Reason & thyself at Strife ;
>   Give anxious Cares & endless Wishes room
> But thro' the cool sequester'd Vale of Life
>   Pursue the silent Tenour of thy Doom.

' And here the Poem was originally intended to conclude, before the happy idea of the hoary-headed Swain, &c., suggested itself to him.' (Mason.)

Some of the phrases he was able to use in his final version, but he could find no place for the beautiful third stanza and, with his scrupulous care for design, refused to make one. Compare the similar instance at l. 116.

l. 78. *still erected* : always erected.

ll. 85–92. A reflection upon the fact, noted in the preceding stanzas, that even the humblest of mankind try to perpetuate themselves by monuments and inscriptions. ' For who, even when death's hand was upon his very speech and memory, ever turned to die without regret for the pleasures and anxieties which fill human life, and without a desire to retain the human sympathy that he found there ? Why ! the instinct is so strong that even from the tomb itself, nay, even from our very ashes, it manages to find expression.' (Witness the ' uncouth rhymes ' and inscriptions by which even these insignificant and ignorant dead strive to preserve their identity.)

l. 100. In Gray's original draft this line was followed by the following stanza :

> Him have we seen the Green-wood Side along
> While o'er the Heath we hied, our Labours done,
> Oft as the Woodlark piped his farewell Song
> With whistful Eyes pursue the setting Sun.

' I rather wonder that he rejected this stanza, as it not only has the same sort of Doric delicacy which charms us peculiarly in this part of the poem, but also completes the account of his whole day : whereas, this evening scene being omitted, we have only his morning walk, and his noontide repose.' (Mason.) Gray probably rejected it as being merely descriptive. ' As to description,' he writes to Dr. Beattie, ' I have always thought it made the most graceful ornament of poetry but never ought to make the subject.'

l. 116. ' Between this line and the Epitaph Mr. Gray originally inserted a very beautiful stanza which was printed in some of the first editions, but afterwards omitted ; because he thought (and in my own opinion very justly) that it was too long a parenthesis in this place. The lines however are in themselves exquisitely fine, and demand preservation.' (Mason.) It was printed thus :

> There scatter'd oft, the earliest of the Year,
> By Hands unseen, are show'rs of Violets found ;
> The Red-breast loves to build and warble there,
> And little Footsteps lightly print the Ground.

This stanza was first printed in the third edition, 1751, and was omitted in 1753.

NOTES ON THE LETTERS

I.

PAGE **69.** Richard West, son of the Lord Chancellor of Ireland, had been one of Gray's chief friends at Eton. He was now in residence at Christ Church, whence he removed to the Temple to study law, but died of consumption in 1742, aged 26. Gray's name for him was Favonius.

l. 11. *my own time . . . reformation.* West's grandfather on the mother's side was Bishop Burnet, who wrote *A History of his own Time*, 1724, and *A History of the Reformation of the Church of England*, 1679.

II.

PAGE **70,** l. 14. *mathematics.* Gray's early editors, Mason and Mitford, try to explain away his contempt for ' this valuable and inestimable science '. But a contempt for mathematics is a well-known undergraduate affectation.

l. 22. *Cambridge.* ' At the time when he was admitted Jacobitism, and its concomitant, hard drinking, prevailed still at Cambridge, much to the prejudice not only of good manners but of good letters.' (Mason.)

l. 23. *the prophet* : Isaiah, chaps. xiii, xxxii, xxxiv.

PAGE **71,** l. 13. *refined friendships.* ' Perhaps he meant to ridicule the affected manner of Mrs. Rowe's letters of the dead to the living.' (Mason.) The letters (*Friendship in Death,* 1728) are a kind of religious sensationalism ; e. g. Letter IX, *To Sylvia from Alexis* : ' From the fragrant bowers, the ever blooming fields and lightsome regions of the Morning Star, I wish health and every blessing to the charming Sylvia, the blessing of the earth. I have a secret to reveal to you, of the greatest importance to your present and future happiness. You are as much a stranger to your own rank and circumstances as I was to mine till I came here ; where I met a fair spirit who informed me, that when she was a mortal I was her son, and not the heir of the Earl of —, as was supposed ; and that the Lord — is your own brother,' &c. From which it appears that in Mrs. Rowe's Heaven they enjoyed the advantages not only of ' refined friendships ' but of highly entertaining scandal.

III.

PAGE **71,** l. 21. *what you sent me last* : an elegy in Latin *Ad Amicos.*

IV.

PAGE **72.** Horace Walpole (1717–97), the famous virtuoso and letter-writer, was the fourth son of Sir Robert, the great Whig minister of George II. Like Gray and West he was an Etonian, and at the date of this letter was an undergraduate of King's College, Cambridge.

l. 20. *Uncle's*: Robert Antrobus of Burnham, Bucks.

PAGE **73,** l. 26. *Southern*: Thomas Southerne (1660–1746), the dramatist, whose *Oroonoko* and *The Fatal Marriage* (of which the heroine is Isabella) held the stage for more than a generation after his death.

V.

PAGE **74.** Walpole was staying at Houghton with his father, whose manners and tastes resembled those of Fielding's Squire Western.

l. 24. *lanthorn*: A gilt lantern for eighteen candles hung in the hall at Houghton, and was often mentioned in Tory satires.

l. 27. *hogan,* or ' hogen mogen ', slang for strong drink, borrowed from Dutch.

VI.

PAGE **75,** l. 29. *Lord Conway* and his brother, General Frances Conway, were Walpole's cousins, whom they had met in Paris.

VIII.

PAGE **80,** l. 31. *St. Bruno*: founder of the monastery, 1086.

l. 35. *Abelard and Heloïse.* Peter Abelard, a great scholar of Paris in the twelfth century, gained the affections of Héloïse, the daughter of a canon. Compelled to separate, the lovers renounced the world. Abelard became a religious ascetic, and founded the convent of the Paraclete, at Nogent on the Seine: Héloïse, who had taken the veil, became its first Abbess. Her famous letters were written at the convent, and both the lovers were buried there. Gray must have been thinking of Pope's romantic poem on the subject, for Nogent is in comparatively flat country.

PAGE **82,** l. 23. *permission*: ' a phrase borrowed from Madame de Sévigné, who quotes a bon mot on Pélisson, " qu'il abusoit la permission qu'ont les hommes d'être laids ".' (Mason.)

IX.

PAGE **82.** Thomas Wharton, M.D., of Old Park, Durham, was a fellow of Pembroke College, Cambridge.

PAGE **86,** l. 33. *the Pretender*: James Edward (1688–1766) the ' old ' Pretender, then resident in Rome. In a later letter to his mother from Rome Gray writes: ' This letter (like all those the English send or receive) will pass through the hands of that Family, before it comes to those it was intended for.'

X.

PAGE **89,** l. 6. *Roman town* : Herculaneum, overwhelmed in A. D. 79.

XI.

PAGE **89.** West had written to say that he had given up all thought of the law as a profession, and that he was in great distress of mind : ' Dear Gray ! consider me in the condition of one that has lived these two years without any person that he can speak freely to. I know it is very seldom that people trouble themselves with the sentiments of those they converse with : so they can chat about trifles they never care whether your heart aches or no. Are you one of these ? I think not.'

PAGE **92,** l. 20. *Epistle to Mr. Ashton* : a verse letter by Walpole. The *Imitation of Spenser* is a poem in Spenserian stanzas by Gilbert West (1705–56), ' On the Abuse of Travelling.'

XII.

PAGE **94,** l. 20. *poetical farewell* : Latin verses of farewell to Florence printed by Mason.

XIII.

PAGE **94.** West, who was now in the last stages of consumption, had sent Gray some humorous Latin verses on his cough.

PAGE **95,** l. 6. *Dunciad* : i. e. *The New Dunciad* by Pope, published 1742 (Book IV of *The Dunciad*).

l. 9. *Joseph Andrews* : by Fielding, published two months previously.

l. 25. *Marivaux* (1688–1763), *Crébillon* the younger (1707–77) : chief writers of the realistic novel in France at this period. ' As to Crebillon, 'twas his " Egaremens du Cœur et de l'Esprit " that our author chiefly esteemed : he had not at this time published his more licentious pieces.' (Mason.)

l. 27. *harangues* : passages from his unfinished tragedy, *Agrippina*, which he had sent to West for his criticism. West had replied that the speech appeared to him too long and the style ' too antiquated '.

XIV.

PAGE **97.** The last of the letters that West received. When Gray wrote again, enclosing the ' Ode on the Spring ', he was dead.

PAGE **98,** l. 14. *Harry the Fourth's supper of Hens* : referring to the old story, told in *Les Cent Nouvelles Nouvelles,* of how a prince retaliated upon his confessor, who had reproved him for his amours, by giving him nothing to eat but his favourite dish. In later versions the hero is Henri Quatre.

l. 22. *Et Caput* : Propertius, iii. 5. 22.

XV.

PAGE **99.** Describes the reconciliation between Gray and Walpole after the quarrel which had occurred at Reggio in 1741. Walpole wrote later : ' The quarrel between Gray and me arose from his being too serious a companion. I had just broke loose from the restraint of the University with as much money as I could spend ; and I was willing to indulge myself. Gray was for antiquities &c., whilst I was for perpetual balls and plays :—the fault was mine.' (Walpoliana.) But it is certain that mischief was made by Thomas Ashton, an Etonian and Cambridge man whom Gray never liked. See D. C. Tovey's *Gray and his Friends*, 1890, pp. 11–13.

XVI.

PAGE **100,** l. 25. *our defeat,* at Falkirk, 17 January 1746 : retrieved by *the Duke* of Cumberland at Culloden. The Pretender's army had penetrated as far as Derby in December.

XVII.

PAGE **102,** l. 1. *Mr. Brown* was the Rev. James Brown, fellow and subsequently Master of Pembroke College, Cambridge, and one of Gray's executors.

l. 28. *Poem of your young friend : The Pleasures of Imagination,* 1744, by Mark Akenside (1721–70), a native of Newcastle.

PAGE **103,** l. 10. *Hutcheson* : Francis Hutcheson (1694–1746), a philosopher of note, author of *An Inquiry into our Ideas of Beauty and Virtue.*

l. 16. *The Enthusiast, or the Lover of Nature,* a poem by Joseph Warton (1722–1800).

l. 18. *The Art of Preserving Health,* 1744, a didactic poem by John Armstrong, M.D. (1709–79).

l. 19. *Tommy Lucretius* : a pet name for the Latin poem *De Principiis Cogitandi,* which Gray never completed.

l. 24. *tar-water* : a universal specific made fashionable by Bishop Berkeley's philosophical work, *Siris,* 1744.

XVIII.

PAGE **104.** The Earl of Kilmarnock and Lord Balmerino were beheaded on 18th of August, and Lord Lovat on the following 16th of April. Cromartie was reprieved and pardoned. For an account of Balmerino's gallant demeanour during the trial see Walpole's letter to Mann of the same date.

XIX.

PAGE **107,** l. 6. *Cibber's book* : Colley Cibber (1671–1757), the actor, playwright, and poet laureate, had just published *The Character and Conduct of Cicero, considered from the History of his Life, by Dr. Middleton,* 1747.

l. 8. *Letitia Pilkington* (1712–50) : an adventuress who owed to Cibber her release from the Marshalsea, where she was imprisoned for debt. Her autobiography (1748) contains reminiscences of Swift, who had befriended her husband.

l. 14. *Daniel Waterland* (1683–1740) : a prominent theologian and controversialist.

l. 30. *Joseph Spence* (1699–1768): the friend of Pope and author of *Polymetis,* 1747, which Gray had read in manuscript.

PAGE **108,** l. 12. *Agrippina* : his tragedy.

l. 18. *the employment you propose* : an edition of his own and of West's poems in a single volume. The project never matured.

l. 23. *This is all* : ' What is here omitted is a short catalogue of Mr. West's poetry then in Gray's hands.' (Mason.)

l. 31. *a few lines* : the apostrophe to West at the beginning of the fourth book of his poem, *De Principiis Cogitandi.*

XX.

PAGE 109. Enclosing ' On the Death of a favourite Cat '.

l. 21. *your new honours* : ' Mr. Walpole was about this time elected a Fellow of the Royal Society.' (Mitford.)

XXI.

PAGE **110,** l. 6. *Dodsley's book* : *A Collection of Poems by Several Hands* (3 vols.) published in January 1748 by Robert Dodsley. In the first edition there is an engraving of the three Graces on the title-page. In the second edition (also 1748) the Graces are replaced by Apollo and the Muses (draped figures), the contents are rearranged, and some forty poems are added. Gray's allusion to the Graces, and the order in which he mentions the authors, make it certain that he was using the first edition, and therefore highly probable that this letter was written early in 1748.

l. 12. *to see myself* : his ' Ode on a Distant Prospect ', ' To Spring ', and ' On the Death of a Favourite Cat ' are printed in vol. ii of the collection.

l. 13. Thomas Tickell (1686–1740) was the friend and literary executor of Addison. The *Collection* begins with his poem *On the Prospect of Peace,* 1712, and his ballad *Colin and Lucy.* Matthew Green (1696–1737) follows with *The Spleen* and other pieces. *The School Mistress* is the well-known imitation of Spenser by William Shenstone (1714–63).

PAGE **111,** l. 1. *London* and the *Prologue spoken by Mr. Garrick at the Opening of the Theatre in Drury Lane,* 1747, are

by Samuel Johnson. John Dyer (1698–1758) is represented
by his best poem *Grongar Hill* and his *Ruins of Rome*. James
Bramston's *Art of Politics* and Dr. William King's *Art of
Cookery* are imitations of Horace's *Ars Poetica*, the former
ambitious, the latter arch, both tedious. Dr. Abel Evans's
Pre-existence, in imitation of Milton, concludes vol. i.

Vol. ii opens with *The Progress of Love* and other poems
by the Hon. George Lyttelton (1709–73). The *Ode to William
Pultney* by Robert Nugent (1702–88), afterwards Earl Nugent,
was supposed to have been written by David Mallet. William
Whitehead (1715–85), poet laureate in 1757, contributes
several pieces. Isaac Hawkins Browne is represented by
A Pipe of Tobacco, a series of six amusing parodies. ˙ Towards
the end of the volume are Horace Walpole's *Epistle from
Florence, written in the year 1740* (i. e. 'your epistle'), and
The Beauties, an Epistle to Mr. Eckardt the Painter.

PAGE **112,** l. 2. Gray here passes to vol. iii, which begins
with *The Choice of Hercules* by Robert Lowth (1710–87),
Professor of Poetry at Oxford, afterwards Bishop of London.
The *sickly Peer* is Lord John Hervey (1696–1743), Pope's
'gilded bug', who in an Epistle (p. 246) moralizes upon the
animals. Soame Jenyns (1704–87), whose *Inquiry into the
Nature and Origin of Evil* was answered by Johnson, contributes among other poems *An Essay on Virtue*, from which
(p. 206) Gray takes the quotation. The volume concludes with
William Mason's *Ode to a Water-Nymph* ; his *Musaeus,
A Monody to the Memory of Mr. Pope*, is in the same volume.

l. 19. *who poor West was* : referring to *A Monody on the
Death of Queen Caroline* ' by Richard West, Esq. ; Son of the
Chancellor of Ireland, and Grandson of Bishop Burnet '
(vol. ii, p. 269). This was to distinguish him from Gilbert
West, author of *The Abuse of Travelling* and *The Order of
the Garter* (vol. ii, pp. 63–154).

l. 21. *Lady Mary*, i. e. Lady Mary Wortley Montagu (1690–
1762), the famous letter-writer, whose *Town Eclogues* are
included in vol. iii of the first edition, in vol. i of the second.

l. 24. *Sir Thomas Fitz-Osborne's Letters*, 1748, a collection of
insipid letters addressed to 'Cleora', 'Hortensius', 'Timoclea',
&c., by William Melmoth.

l. 33. *The thinking sculpture* : from Matthew Green's
The Grotto.

XXII.

PAGE **113.** Gray's aunt, Mrs. Mary Antrobus, had died on
5 November.

XXIII.

PAGE **114.** Enclosing the 'Elegy'.

PAGE **115,** l. 22. *Middleton*: Conyers Middleton (1683–1750), a well-known Deist. In a letter to Walpole Gray writes : ' You have doubtless heard of the loss I have had in Dr. Middleton, whose house was the only easy place one could find to converse in at Cambridge. For my part I find a friend so uncommon a thing that I cannot help regretting even an old acquaintance.' (9 August 1750.) See note on p. 107, l. 6.

XXIV.

PAGE **115.** See note (p. 164) on the *Elegy*.

XXV.

PAGE **116,** l. 26. *a pinch or two* : i. e. misprints.

PAGE **117,** l. 7. *a drama* : *Elfrida*, by William Mason (1724–97), fellow of Pembroke College, Cambridge, subsequently a canon of York, who edited Gray's works in 1775.

XXVI.

PAGE **118,** l. 1. *the print* : the engraving of a village funeral which Bentley had designed for the ' Elegy '.

XXVII.

PAGE **119,** l. 9. *Strawberry-castle* : Walpole's villa at Strawberry Hill, which he had furnished in what he believed to be pure Gothic taste (see Letter XXXV).

l. 13. *Lord Radnor.* His neighbour, Lord Radnor, had put up ' a Chinese summer house ', and his ' garden was full of statues, &c., like that at Marylebone '. Walpole thought him mad, and called his garden ' Mabland '.

XXIX.

PAGE **125,** l. 3. *Lisbon* : Voltaire's poem *La Destruction de Lisbonne*.

l. 13. *Man-Midwives* : ' The Reviewers, at the time, were supposed to be of these professions.' (Mason.) Perhaps a reference to Tobias Smollett, M.D., founder and editor of *The Critical Review*, 1756. *Presbyterian Parsons* : i. e. the staff of *The Monthly Review*.

l. 25. *fantasies* : Mason had sent him a sketch of his tragedy, *Caractacus*.

PAGE **126,** l. 3. *glorious successes* : the loss of Minorca in June, owing to the misconduct of Admiral Byng.

XXX.

PAGE **126.** Richard Hurd (1719–1808), fellow of Emmanuel College, Cambridge, subsequently Bishop of Lichfield and of Worcester, author of *Letters on Chivalry and Romance*, 1762. Gray had made him a present of the two Odes.

XXXI.

PAGE 128, l. 17. *my List*: 'A catalogue of the Antiquities, Houses, &c., in England and Wales which Gray drew up in the blank pages of Kitchin's English Atlas.' (Mitford.)

l. 22. *Mrs. Cibber* (1714–66), the celebrated actress and sister of the composer, Dr. Arne, took the part of Evanthe in Garrick's production of the tragedy of *Agis*, by John Home (1722–1808, author of *Douglas*), on 21st February, the date of this letter. Her *canary-bird* is probably her brother's favourite pupil, Charlotte Brent (d. 1802), who made her first appearance as a singer in this month, but was refused an engagement by Garrick. This may be the 'misfortune' to which Gray alludes.

l. 26. *Swift's* ' History of the Four Last Years of the Queen ' (an account of the negotiations leading to the Peace of Utrecht) was published posthumously in 1758.

l. 27. *Stuart's Attica*: 'The Antiquities of Athens Delineated ', 1762, by James Stuart, a well-known architect.

XXXII.

PAGE 129. William Palgrave, a Fellow of Pembroke College, Cambridge, was making a tour in Scotland.

XXXIII.

PAGE 130, l. 18. *Caradoc*: Mason's *Caractacus*, with the choric Odes inserted.

l. 20. *the Dragon of Wantley's Dam*: Gray's aunt, Mrs. Oliffe, whom he found difficult. She had been appointed joint executor with Gray by his other aunt, Mrs. Rogers. The reference is to Carey's burlesque opera of 1737, called *The Dragon of Wantley*, and founded on an old Yorkshire legend.

XXXIV.

PAGE 132, l. 11. *Dr. Templeman*: Keeper of the Reading Room at the British Museum, 1758–61.

l. 16. *Dr. Pocock*: Richard Pocock (1704–65), afterwards Bishop of Meath, a great traveller and topographer.

l. 17. *Dr. Stukeley*: William Stukeley (1687–1765), the eccentric antiquary and authority on the Druids.

l. 26. *Clarendon's* autobiography was published in 1759.

l. 27. *Mr. Cambridge*: Richard Owen Cambridge (1717–1802), a poet, wit, and journalist, admired by Horace Walpole. He wrote *The Scribleriad*, 1751, a satire on false taste.

XXXV.

PAGE 133, l. 22. *Stonehewer*: Richard Stonehewer (1728–1809) a fellow of Peterhouse, had been tutor to the Duke of Grafton, and was appointed Historiographer Royal in 1755. Gray's private papers were bequeathed to him by William Mason, and by him presented to Pembroke College, Cambridge.

XXXVI.

PAGE **135.** Gray had just returned from a visit to Lady Cobham. Dr. Clarke was his physician.

PAGE **136,** l. 5. *Dr. Chapman*: Master of Magdalene College, Cambridge.

l. 14. *Erse Fragments*: 'Fragments of Ancient Poetry, collected in the Highlands of Scotland, and translated from the Galic or Erse Language', 1760, by James Macpherson.

XL.

PAGE **140.** Mr. Brown was now Master of Pembroke College: see note on Letter XVII. Mr. Howe was an honorary Fellow, resident in Brussels.

PAGE **141,** l. 13. *Ossian*: the bard whose poems Macpherson professed to have translated. See Letter XXXVI.

XLI.

PAGE **141.** Count Algarotti (1712–64) was a distinguished Italian, chamberlain to the King of Prussia, and author of treatises on Painting, on the Opera, and on the French Academy for Painters in Italy. These he had sent to Gray, by the hands of Mr. Howe, with a panegyric on the Odes.

XLII.

PAGE **145.** Norton Nicholls (1742?–1809) of Trinity Hall, Cambridge ; Gray's youthful friend and pupil, who became Rector of Lound, near Lowestoft, in 1767, and wrote valuable 'Reminiscences of Gray', printed by Mitford.

XLIV

PAGE **147,** l. 23. *Mr. Bentley's designs*: i. e. for the 1753 edition. See p. xi and Letter XXVI.

PAGE **149,** l. 1. *Boswell's book*: 'An Account of Corsica, the Journal of a Tour to that Island, and Memoirs of Pascal Paoli', 1768, by Johnson's biographer.

XLVI.

PAGE **151,** l. 13. *Odicle*: The 'Ode for Music on the Duke of Grafton's Installation'.

l. 15. *North Briton*: the organ of Wilkes and his faction.

l. 26. *Shenstone's Letters*: the third or supplementary volume of his Works, published 1769.

JOURNAL.

PAGE **154,** l. 25. *Non ragioniam*: Dante, *Inferno*, iii. 51.

PAGE **156,** l. 12. *Pennant*: Thomas Pennant (1726–98) the distinguished naturalist, had published the first part of his *British Zoology* in 1766.

l. 27. *dark to me*: Milton, *Samson Agonistes*, ll. 86–9.